REEDY

REEDY

ONE-HUNDRED-SEVENTEENTH IN A SERIES OF JESS WILLIAMS WESTERNS

ROBERT J. THOMAS

Copyright© 2022 by Robert J. Thomas

All rights reserved, including the right to reproduce this book or portions thereof in any form. No part of this text may be reproduced, transmitted, downloaded, decompiled, or stored into or introduced into any electronic or mechanical method without the written permission of the author and/or publisher. The scanning, uploading and distribution of this book via the Internet or via any other means without the written permission of the author and/or publisher is illegal and punishable by law.

This book is a work of fiction. Names, characters, places and incidents are either the product of the author's imagination or are used fictitiously. Any resemblance to actual events, locales, organizations, or persons living or dead is entirely coincidental and beyond the intent of either the author and/or publisher. They are solely the imagination of the author and/or publisher and the imagination of events that may or may not possibly happen.

A Jess Williams Novel
Westerns. Revenge. Violence. Action. Adventure.
ISBN Paperback: 978-1-955914-12-3

DEDICATION

As my readers know, Frank Reedy, is a mainstay character in my Jess Williams Western Series. What you may not know, is Reedy is based on my very dear friend, Mike Reddy, who is depicted on the cover of this book.

Mike has been a true and loyal friend for more years than I can count. He is the kind of friend who is always there, in the best of times and the worst of times.

He has been at my side throughout the years, always ready to help and pitch in when the going got tough.

"Mike, this book is dedicated to you for all your help and friendship over the years."

CHAPTER ONE

Jess had finished his special assignments from United States Marshal Frank Reedy and was back to doing what he did best, hunting down the worst of killers and sending them to their graves.

He had camped about ten miles outside the town of Alger, Texas. The cold-blooded killer he was on the hunt for was Jim Fisk, who had murdered four people so far. Jess didn't want to see a fifth victim at the hands of Fisk.

After eating a sparse meal of beans with pieces of beef jerky and a cut-up onion in it, Jess sat by his fire, sipping coffee and waiting for the pan bread to finish cooking.

He had added raisins and some fresh blueberries he'd picked outside his camp earlier when he was putting up cans with strings around the perimeter.

While he watched the bread cooking, he thought about Jim Fisk. When it was done, he took the bread out and let it cool a little before eating half of it. After he finished, he doused the fire with water from one of his canteens.

Crawling into his bedroll, he fell off to sleep with his pistol on his stomach.

***

The town of Alger was small. It had one saloon, one general store and two liveries, although one was vacant and closed for business. The little hotel consisted of only four rooms, but it had a small café inside.

The hotel was owned by an older woman by the name of Gracie. She provided all the food for the Alger Saloon. The saloon and the café were only four feet apart.

The owner of the saloon had run a string on rollers from the saloon to the café. He would jot down the orders, clip them to the string and send them to the café.

Gracie had a younger boy by the name of Toby working for her. He waited on tables and ran the food orders over to the saloon. Gracie always made some type of soup or stew to stay on the stove in the saloon and be served by the owner and barkeep, Eleby Shore.

It was late in the afternoon when Shore heard the door creak open upstairs. A few seconds later, his only guest was walking down the steps.

Jim Fisk wore a gun belt that held a Colt pistol tied down tight and low on his right leg. On his left hip, he wore a large bowie knife in a sheath. He was a man of average build and height, with a stubbly face that rarely smiled and a pudgy nose.

He reached the bottom of the steps and moved to the bar. The barkeep knew he liked brandy. He poured some into a glass and slid it to him.

"What's in the pot today?" Fisk asked.

"Venison stew with vegetables," answered the barkeep.

"That's what you had yesterday."

"Didn't serve that much of it," Shore explained. "I kept it on the stove all night and added fresh vegetables today. It's better than yesterday. Meat is more tender."

"You got some fresh bread to go with it?"

"No, but I can get some in a minute or so."

He jotted down a note, walked to the wall, pinned it to the string and sent it to the café. When it arrived, Gracie snatched it off the string and looked at it.

"Toby, take another loaf of bread to the saloon," she told him.

He jumped out of his seat, grabbed a fresh loaf and put it into a basket. He ran out of the café and over to the saloon.

"Here's the bread you ordered," said Toby.

"Thanks Toby," said the barkeep as he took the basket.

Toby turned and gazed at the rough-looking man standing at the bar, a scowl on his face.

Fisk took a sip of his whiskey and set the glass down when he noticed the boy staring at him.

"What you lookin' at, you little shit?" he asked in a gruff voice.

Toby simply shook his head and headed for the batwings. Fisk watched him and grunted.

The barkeep walked out with the stew and two thick slices of the bread. He set it down in front of him and smiled. The barkeep shook his head.

"He's a good boy," he said. "Works hard and he'll do anything you ask of him."

"Good, then ask him to stay out of my sight," spat Fisk.

The barkeep sighed and headed to the kitchen to stir the pot. Fisk ate his stew and sipped his whiskey. He stayed downstairs and watched the local men, playing cards or just drinking and talking while eating the stew. After a while, he returned to his room for the night.

***

Jess woke at the first signs of daylight. He made coffee and ate the rest of the pan bread. He figured he could reach the town of Alger soon enough and he would eat there, Fisk or no Fisk.

After collecting his cans, he rode out of the camp and onto the trail that would lead him to town. After a while, he saw the town up ahead on the trail. He rode toward the near end of the main street, then stopped and scanned the town for a few minutes.

Seeing neither hide nor hair of his prey, he headed for the livery he had spotted. When he rode to the opening, he dismounted, looked along the main street and then walked his horses inside.

The owner, a bear of a man, walked out and smiled at him.

"Well, if it ain't the infamous bounty hunter, Jess Williams himself. You must be hunting someone. Who might that be?"

Jess took out the wanted poster on Jim Fisk and showed it to him.

He nodded his head.

"Yep, he's been stayin' over at the saloon down the street," he said. "Figured him for a bad one, but didn't know he was a killer wanted by the law."

"Is his horse in here?"

"No, he lit outta here after his morning meal," he replied. "Said he'd be back later though."

"Did he say where he was going?" Jess asked.

"Uh, no, he didn't."

"What's around town?"

"Not much. A half dozen small houses, a small sheep farmer, a few dirt farmers, one pig farmer who supplies smoked hams, bacon, and the like. That's about it. Closest town is almost a day's ride from here, so if he was going there, he wouldn't be coming back later today."

"Who serves food in town?"

"The saloon and the café in the hotel," he explained. "I'd go to the café myself. Gracie cooks most of the food for the saloon anyway."

"Thanks, I'll do that," said Jess.

"What do you want me to do with your horses?"

"For now, just feed and water them," he said as he pitched the man a five-dollar gold piece.

He grinned widely.

"Thanks, Mr. Williams," he said.

Jess walked out and looked around. The town had seen better days. Some of the buildings looked run-down and others were boarded up. He saw the saloon and the café next to it. He walked past the saloon to the café.

He stopped when he saw a slip of paper moving between the two buildings on a string. It came out of a hole in the wall of the saloon and disappeared into a hole in the wall of the café.

"That's interesting," he said as he headed for the door of the café.

When he walked inside, he was surprised by the fact that almost all the patrons eating were women. Only two men sat at tables with women.

The place was small, but clean. There were only six tables in the serving area and behind that was a doorway and open window going to the kitchen.

Near the doorway, a young boy sat on a chair. He was watching people eating. A woman's head popped out the window of the kitchen.

"Toby, another platter of bacon for the saloon," she said.

Toby jumped from his chair, ran into the kitchen, and came out with a platter of fried bacon. He ran past Jess, glancing up at him as he did. He went out and headed for the saloon.

"Bacon cooked exactly the way I like it," Jess said to himself.

Everyone was looking at him curiously. One of the men looked over at him.

"Most men eat over at the saloon," he offered politely.

"Is there a reason I can't eat here?" Jess asked.

The man looked at the other man in the place. They both shrugged their shoulders.

"Uh, I can't think of one," he said.

Gracie popped her head out through the window and saw him standing there with all his guns.

"You gonna cause me any trouble?" she asked in a stern voice.

"No, ma'am," he said, "I'm just hungry and your food looks delicious."

"Well then, have a seat and give Toby your order when he returns," she said.

"Yes, ma'am."

He sat at a table where he could see the door of the café.

Toby came in and stopped at his table.

"How come you got all them guns, mister?" he asked.

"I'm a bounty hunter, and these are my tools."

"Oh, well, do you want something to eat?"

"Scrambled eggs, crispy bacon and fried potatoes."

"Okay," Toby said as he ran into the kitchen.

He came out a minute later with a plate of food and a cup of coffee. He set it on the table and went back to his chair.

Jess picked up a piece of bacon and took a bite.

"This is delicious," he said.

Gracie popped her head out and smiled at him.

"Of course, it is," she said.

CHAPTER TWO

Herman Ladd and his wife, Harriet, were out in the corn field picking ears of corn. Both wore large straw hats to protect their faces and eyes from the sun.

Herman filled his basket and looked over at his wife.

"Harriet, did you fill your basket yet?"

She looked over the corn stalks.

"Just a few more," she said as she brushed her hair back behind her shoulder.

"I'm gonna go and get the mule hooked up to the wagon to take this stuff to town with the tomatoes, carrots, and taters. Dom should be here any minute now."

Herman walked out of the tall cornfield to see a man sitting on his horse, watching them.

"Mister, are you lost?" Herman asked.

"No, I was just riding around the town and saw all the vegetables you got growin' here," he said. "I was wondering if you'd sell me some taters and corn."

Reedy

"Sure," said Herman. "Come on over to the wagon and pick out what you want before I take it to town."

"Thanks," said the man as he slid from the saddle.

He followed Herman to his wagon and Herman put the corn on the back of it. He turned to the man to say something, but the man plunged a bowie knife into his stomach and twisted it, while covering Herman's mouth with his other hand.

He pulled out the knife. Herman's knees gave out and he slumped to the ground. His hat rolled off his head. Blood trickled from the corner of his lips as his last breath escaped his lungs.

Jim Fisk stood over Herman and waited for that last breath. Then, he reached down and picked up the straw hat, removed his own and put on Herman's hat.

Leaving his hat on the wagon, he headed for the cornfield where Harriet was still picking corn. He walked into the cornfield.

She saw the hat moving amid the corn tassels and smiled.

"Did you come to help me, dear?" she asked as she looked at the ears, trying to decide which ones were the best to pick.

Fisk coughed instead of answering. He moved closer to her and when there was only one row of stalks between them, she finally looked up at him. Her face soured.

"You're not Herman," she said.

"I hope not," he said as he moved forward and swung his arm, slashing her throat with the bowie knife.

She fell through the next few rows of stalks, collapsing onto the ground. He walked through the stalks and stood over her as she was attempting to take her last gasping, gurgling breaths.

He leaned down and wiped the blade on her plaid shirt and then slid it back into the sheath on his left hip.

He walked to the house and entered. Going into the bedroom first, he rifled through the tallboy and under some shirts in the middle drawer. He found their hidden cash. He counted out eighty-five dollars and stuffed it into his front pocket.

Feeling he had found all their savings, he walked out and strode to the wagon, where Herman still lay, his dead eyes staring at the clear blue sky.

Picking up a tomato, he bit into it and chewed. He swallowed it and toed Herman's dead body.

"Damn tasty tomato," he said. "Too bad they're not gettin' them in town."

He threw the straw hat down onto Herman's face, donned his own hat and walked to his horse. After climbing up in the saddle, he finished eating the tomato and sleeved his mouth. Turning his horse around, he casually headed back to Alger, purposely taking the long way around.

Not a half hour later, Dom, a friend of Herman and Harriet Ladd, rode toward the Ladds' farm. Dom was a single man and grew vegetables too, although they had a gentleman's agreement to grow different produce.

Dom grew melons, watermelons, cucumbers, squash, onions, and a few other vegetables. When he got closer, he saw the wagon, but the mule wasn't hooked up, which he thought odd.

Then, as he rode closer, he saw the body on the ground behind the wagon. The straw hat was still over the face.

"What the hell, Herman," muttered Dom. "You taking a nap now?"

He rode closer. When he got close enough, he saw the large bloodstain on Herman's shirt. He halted the wagon, jumped out and ran to Herman. He bent over and removed the straw hat.

"Oh, Herman, who did this to you?"

He thought about Harriet and stood up.

"Harriet," he yelled as he looked around excitedly.

The front door of the house was open, so he headed straight for it. He went inside and saw no one in the main room.

He went into the bedroom and noticed the middle drawer of the tallboy open and the clothes scattered on the floor. He knew that was where Herman kept his life savings. Going to it, he saw that the money was gone.

Seeing no signs of Harriet in the house anywhere, he went outside and started looking around the farm. When he started walking through the cornfield, he noticed the two legs on the ground, protruding through the stalks.

He parted the cornstalks and walked to the spot. When he saw Harriet on the ground with her throat slashed, he whimpered and shook his head.

"Oh, Harriet," he whispered through his hands covering his mouth. "Who could have done such a horrible thing?"

He went inside the house and came back out with two blankets. After covering their bodies to protect them from the sun, he looked over at their wagon.

He transferred their load of vegetables to his wagon, figuring he could use the proceeds to help bury his two friends.

He pushed his mule as hard as he could to reach town. When he arrived, he headed straight for the saloon. There was no law in Alger, but the saloon seemed to be the hub for the small town.

Jess was still sitting in the café, relaxing, and waiting for Fisk to return. He saw the wagon pull up out outside and watched the man jump from the seat and run into the saloon.

He placed a five-dollar gold piece on his table, donned his hat and stood up. Before he reached the door, Toby was standing at his table, holding the coin.

"Hey mister, don't you want your change?" Toby asked.

Jess swiveled his head over his shoulders at him.

"Naw, the food was that good," he said. "And half of that is yours."

"Thanks, mister," he said as he headed to the kitchen to tell Gracie.

Jess walked outside and over to the saloon, slipping his hammer strap off before he went inside. Several men were congregated around the barkeep, talking among themselves.

"Well, all we can do now is go out and bury them," said the barkeep. "Sam, you go wire the county sheriff about what happened and he'll come and investigate. Tell everyone in town

Reedy

I'm taking up a collection for their burials. If we get enough, maybe we can get coffins and grave markers for them. If not, a rug or pine box will have to do."

The men all dispersed, walking around Jess and heading out of the saloon. Jess walked to the barkeep, who kept shaking his head, a saddened expression on his face. He noticed Jess standing there.

"Oh, sorry, what can I do for ya, Mr. Williams?" asked the barkeep.

"You know who I am?"

"Liveryman couldn't wait to tell us who you were."

"Who don't you tell me what happened?"

"Oh, a farmer and his wife were murdered this morning," he explained. "Stabbed to death. Such nice people, everyone in town loved them. Dom, another farmer, found them and came into town to tell us the horrible news. Whoever done it took all their money too. We just don't know who would do such a thing."

"I have an idea who it might have been," said Jess.

"Huh?" asked the barkeep with a shocked expression rippling across his face.

CHAPTER THREE

Jess took out the wanted poster on Jim Fisk and showed it to him.

The barkeep tapped on it.

"This man is staying in one of my rooms upstairs," he said. "You think he might have done it?"

"The liveryman said he left this morning and told him he was coming back. He is a cold-blooded murderer, so yeah, I think so."

"Well, what are you gonna do about it?"

"This husband and wife who were just murdered, where is their place?"

"A few miles out of town that way," he said, pointing.

"I'm going out there to take a look around," said Jess. "If this man comes back in here, don't act suspicious or ask him any questions. Wait until I get back. He's a very dangerous man and he'd just as soon kill you as argue with you."

"Okay, I can do that," the barkeep said.

Jess put the wanted poster back into his pocket and headed to the livery. He climbed up on Gray and rode his horses out of the livery doors.

Riding to the end of the main street, he began following the wagon ruts that Dom had just made coming into town, knowing that they would lead to the murdered couple's house.

As he rode, he noticed one set of hoof prints going toward the house. He made note of them and continued until he saw the house up ahead.

He reined up next to the wagon where the one body lay, covered with a blanket. He rode around the front of the house and dismounted.

After going inside and finding no one, he walked outside and finally found the woman on the ground in the cornfield, a blanket covering her body.

He walked back to the front of the house and looked at the hoof prints. He saw the ruts for the wagon and the mule pulling it away from the house. He also found the same single set of horseshoe prints approaching the house and leaving.

After climbing up in the saddle on Gray, he began following the tracks leaving. They soon turned outward and seemed to be going in a wide circle.

He decided that if the tracks belonged to the man he thought it was, they would come back around toward the town, so he cut straight across the grassy field.

Back in Alger, Jim Fisk rode casually into the livery. The word had spread about the murders along with directions that no one should mention it to the drifter who had been staying in town.

Fisk noticed the cold expression on the liveryman's face as he handed his horse's reins to him.

"Something wrong?" Fisk asked him.

He looked up at him.

"Oh, got one of them damn toothaches in the back," he lied. "It's killin' me."

"Best to just get it pulled," said Fisk.

"Yeah, I'm going to the doc's place soon," he said as he held his cheek.

Fisk took his rifle and headed for the Alger Saloon. When he walked in, the place was quiet. The barkeep stood behind the bar and smiled.

"You want your brandy?" he asked.

Fisk shook his head.

"Gonna take a short nap first. When I come down, make sure you have a better bottle of brandy for me."

"I've got an expensive bottle in the back, but it's twelve dollars," he said.

"I'll pay for it when I come down," said Fisk.

"All right," said the barkeep.

Fisk went upstairs and closed his door. The barkeep went to the back room and found the bottle of brandy. He picked it up and examined it.

"Probably paying for it with Herman and Harriet's money," he whispered to himself.

Reedy

***

When Jess got close to the town, the same tracks veered back to the main trail. He followed them to the end of the street where they got lost in all the other tracks.

He headed straight for the livery, keeping his head down and his eyes wide open. When he reached the livery, he rode inside before dismounting. The liveryman walked up to him.

"Did that man I showed you on the wanted poster come back in?" Jess asked.

"Yeah," he said. "Do you think he killed Herman and Harriet?"

"Probably. Which horse is his?"

"This one over here," he said as he started walking toward it.

Jess walked into the stall and lifted each leg and examined the shoes on them. He stood up and looked at the man.

"This horse went to their house and came back to town the long way," said Jess. "I think he's the one who murdered them, but he's already wanted dead or alive, so he's going to his grave today either way. Is he at the saloon now?"

"That's where he went when he left here," said the man.

"Well, that's the last place he's ever going," said Jess. "Stable my horses for me."

"Sure thing," he said.

Jess slipped his hammer strap off and walked out. Heading straight for the saloon, he saw Toby coming out of the café, heading to the saloon. Jess waved his hands over his head.

"Toby," he shouted out.

The boy stopped and looked at him. Jess motioned for him to go back to the café. Toby shrugged his shoulders and looked confused. Jess huffed, gave him a stern warning look and stuck his left arm out, index finger pointing to the café.

Toby, wasn't sure what it meant, but he did turn on his heels and go back into the café. Jess continued to the saloon and quietly took the steps to the batwings. He looked over them and the barkeep pointed to the upstairs.

He nodded that he understood and walked in. Most of the men filtered out of the saloon, with only a few staying to see what would happen.

Jess walked in and went slowly to one end of the bar. The barkeep moved over to him.

"How long has he been up there?"

"About an hour, maybe more," said the barkeep as he looked out at the batwings. "Where is Toby with the sandwich I ordered?"

"Oh, I sent him back in case Fisk was down here," explained Jess.

"Oh, I understand," said the barkeep as he looked at one of the locals still inside.

"You're gonna have to wait on your sandwich," said the barkeep. "You want some bean and ham soup?"

The man nodded. The barkeep went to the kitchen and came out with a bowl of the soup. Jess waited for Fisk to come down from his room. He heard the door creak open upstairs and moved a foot away from the bar.

Reedy

The boots started landing on the top steps at the same instant that Gracie from the café came walking in, a stern look on her face.

"Why did you send Toby back in with that sandwich?" she asked. "It was a hot ham sandwich with some cheese melted on it. Now, I have to remake it, 'cause the cheese ain't melted anymore."

Fisk was down at the bottom of the steps now and he was listening to Gracie complaining and not paying any attention to who was in there.

"Shut yer piehole, woman," he grumbled. "I just woke up and don't need to listen to you griping about cheese."

He turned at the steps and noticed Jess standing there. He didn't know who he was, but he knew by the looks of him that he was either a lawman or bounty hunter.

Gracie went to shake her finger at Fisk, but he grabbed her, spun her around and put his arm around her waist. She struggled, but he was too strong for her.

"Let go of me, you big brute," she cried.

Fisk sneered at Jess as he pulled his Colt from his holster and placed the barrel of it behind her ear. She immediately stopped struggling and Fisk glared at Jess.

"I don't know who you are, but if you think you're taking me in, you are sadly mistaken."

Jess put his left hand out, palm side.

"Don't hurt her," he said, "I'm sure we can make some kind of deal."

Fisk scoffed.

"You've got nothing to deal with, mister," he spat. "Seems like I got all the aces in the deck now."

"Well, I could see where you would think that," Jess told him, taking one step closer, keeping his right hand down by the butt of his unique pistol.

"Mister, I'm not thinkin' it, I know it," he bragged.

"Do you really?" asked Jess as he took one smaller step forward. "I mean, yeah, you could shoot her in the head, but then what? She'll be dead and then I'll just shoot you. But, there's a way out for all of us, at least for now."

"Yeah? How?"

"You let Gracie go, and I'll let you go to the livery and saddle your horse," he explained. "Then, I'll give you a half hour head start after you ride out of the livery before I come after you."

"You'll shoot me the second I let this woman go," argued Fisk. "The only way I stay alive is to keep her as a hostage."

"You're dead wrong about that," advised Jess as he took another small step forward.

"Stop moving toward me," he said as he pressed the barrel harder against her head, causing Gracie to whimper louder.

"All right, I'll stop moving. Just don't hurt her."

"Why do you care so much about this woman anyway? She your wife or sister or something?" demanded Fisk.

"Just met her today, but she's a really good cook," he said, grinning.

Gracie looked scared and frustrated.

Reedy

"Tell him whatever he wants to hear to get him to let go of me," she wailed.

"I'm not gonna lie to him," said Jess. "I don't do that."

"Well, maybe you might think that now is a good time to start," she yelled in a frustrated voice.

"Nah. Once you start lyin' no one has a reason to believe you after that," Jess told her.

"Who the hell are you and why should I believe anything you say?" inquired Fisk.

"The name is Jess Williams. My word is gold."

It took a second or two for the recognition of the name to sink into Fisk's brain, but when it did, he sighed.

"Aw, hell, you'll just hunt me down and kill me anyway," acknowledge Fisk, "I might as well die right here and now."

CHAPTER FOUR

The room stood still, as if frozen in time for a few tense minutes. Jess stayed ready for anything, not knowing what Fisk would really do.

He worried that Fisk would simply shoot Gracie and turn the gun on him, in which case, Jess would kill him first, but at the cost of Gracie's life.

The one thing going in Jess's and Gracie's favor, was the fact that Fisk hadn't pulled the hammer back on his pistol yet. Jess thought of the only thing left to do. He suddenly looked at Gracie directly and jerked his head sideways before straightening it up again.

She narrowed her eyes at him questioningly, as if she didn't understand. Fisk looked confused also. Jess jerked his head one way again, and Fisk looked at him.

"What the hell is wrong with your head?" demanded Fisk.

"Nothing," he answered, as he jerked it sideways again, causing Fisk to huff and look angrier.

"Stop that!" blurted Fisk.

Jess jerked his head sideways again and raised his eyebrows at Gracie.

She finally understood and violently jerked her head sideways and down at the same time. Fisk put his thumb on the hammer to pull it back, but he never made it.

Jess slicked out his gun and fired one shot. The slug slapped Fisk in the forehead, snapping his head back. His left arm fell from Gracie's waist. She screamed and ran toward Jess. Fisk's body slammed onto the saloon floor hard.

Gracie was still screaming when she reached Jess and began pounding on his chest and sobbing uncontrollably.

"You could've got me killed," she moaned.

Slowly, she stopped pounding on his chest. He reached his left arm around her and held her. Her sobbing subsided and she wrapped her arms around him.

"I'm sorry, but it was the only way out," he told her in a soft voice. "He had nothing to live for and he knew I was gonna kill him now or later. All I needed was a cleaner head shot and you gave it to me."

She looked up from his chest with watery eyes.

"But what if you had missed?"

"That's just it, Gracie, I never miss," he told her.

"Really?"

"Never, not when it's that close a distance," he assured her. "Besides, he had finally made the decision to kill you and try to kill me before I got off a clean shot. I saw it in his eyes. It was the only course of action left, honest."

"Well, you scared the shit out of me," she said as she sniffled and let go of him.

"I know, but you'll be all right in a little bit," he assured her.

"No, I mean you really made me shit myself," she said.

Jess sniffed the air and sighed.

"Oh, I'm so sorry," he said.

"I gotta go and clean up," she said.

"What about my ham sandwich?" said the local man.

She shot him a look of admonishment.

"If you want your sandwich right now, it's gonna have something on it you won't like," she told him.

"I guess I can wait," he said sheepishly.

Gracie went out and returned to her place. Jess replaced the spent shell in his pistol and holstered it. He walked over to the body and emptied Fisk's pockets.

He found the eighty-five dollars in one pocket and several dollars and some change in another. He took it to the bar and handed it to the barkeep.

"That should be enough to bury them now," said Jess.

"Yeah," said the barkeep. "I'll send Dom out with the undertaker to pick up the bodies and bring them here so they can be buried in the local cemetery."

Jess looked at the men inside now.

"Two of you take his body to the livery and tell the worker there to have the body ready for transport tomorrow morning," said Jess as he held out a silver dollar in each hand.

Reedy

Two men jumped up, grabbed the money, then the body, and hauled it out of the saloon. Jess looked at the barkeep.

"I'm gonna take a little walk around town and then have supper over at the café," Jess told him.

The barkeep nodded. Jess went outside and saw Toby coming out of the café with the sandwich in his hand again. He stopped in front of Jess and looked up at him curiously.

"Did you kill that man?"

"Yes, but he was a bad man."

"Why did you stop me from going in there?"

"Because you might have caught a stray bullet."

"So, you didn't want me to get hurt?"

"Exactly."

"Well then, I guess I should thank you."

"You're welcome, Toby."

He nodded and went past him and into the saloon. Jess stepped off the boardwalk and started walking around town.

***

The little village of Fulton was a quiet one. It only had one street. There was no law, no jail, not even any officials of the town that consisted of about fifty people or so.

The only barroom was Turk's Saloon. It was owned and run by a man by the name of Turk, a nickname given to him by everyone in town because he ran a small turkey farm.

Turkey was the only main food served in the saloon besides breakfast. Turk, a big burly man, stood behind the bar, talking to one of the local farmers. He heard a horse approaching outside and looked over the batwings to see a man dismounting.

The man wrapped the reins around the hitching rail, slipped his hammer strap off his pistol and looked up and down the street.

He turned and walked up the steps to the boardwalk and gazed over the batwings.

Turk smiled at the man and waved him in.

"Come on in and wet yer whistle, mister," he said.

The man smiled nervously and pushed through the batwings. He was skinny, with a heavily pockmarked face, dark beady eyes, and a crooked nose.

Turk thought the man looked familiar in some way, but he couldn't put a finger on it. The man moseyed up to the bar and set a silver dollar on it.

"Whatcha drinkin'?" Turk asked.

"Whiskey," he said.

Turk got a bottle and a glass. He set the glass in front of him and poured some whiskey into it, all the while eyeballing the man.

"Just passin' through or staying the night?" Turk asked.

"You got rooms for rent cheap?" he asked.

"For one dollar, you get a room, plus two free drinks, supper and breakfast included," he explained.

"Well, what's for supper? It sure smells good comin' from the kitchen."

"The only thing we serve here is turkey, just about any way you want it," Turk bragged with a smile. "Hot turkey sandwiches, sliced turkey, smoked turkey, white meat, dark meat, turkey pies with gravy and vegetables in 'em. You name it and we can cook it. We even have turkey jerky and turkey sausages."

"Turkey for breakfast too?" he asked.

"If you want," said Turk. "But we also serve eggs, bacon, taters, flapjacks and of course, smoked turkey."

The man placed a silver dollar on the bar and Turk handed him a key, his eyes lingering on the man's face for a few extra seconds. He looked over at the man he had been talking to earlier.

"Take over the bar for me for a few minutes," Turk told him.

"Do I get another free whiskey?" asked the man.

"Yeah, you get another free whiskey," said Turk.

Turk went to the kitchen and his friend went behind the bar. His friend got a beer glass and filled it to the top with whiskey.

Back in the kitchen, Turk stirred the pot of turkey stew and checked the turkey in the oven. He put his hands on his hips and stood there, picturing the man's face in his mind.

He sighed and went to his little office off the kitchen and sat down. He opened a drawer in his desk and pulled out some papers. After blowing off the dust, he started going through them one by one.

When he came to the old wanted poster on Ned Malone, the instant recognition slapped him across the face. The man standing at his bar was the same man on the wanted poster he was holding in his hands. He was wanted for one thousand dollars, which was a small fortune.

"Well, I'll be," he whispered to himself.

He reached over in the corner, picked up his double-barreled shotgun and opened the breach to make sure it was loaded. He closed it and went to the back door of the kitchen.

Quietly, he opened the door and went out and around to the front of the saloon. He peeked over the batwings and raised the shotgun up as he pushed through.

"Ned Malone, you are under arrest for murder," bellowed the barkeep.

Malone moved his right hand off the bar, but when he heard the familiar clicking sounds of the two hammers being eared back on the shotgun, he put his right hand back on top of the bar. He looked at the barkeep in the mirror.

"I think you've made a big mistake. That's not my name."

"I got an old wanted poster on my desk in the back that says otherwise," said Turk.

"I don't believe you."

Turk looked over at the man he'd asked to take over the bar. He saw the beer glass filled to the top with whiskey.

Turk shook his head.

"Jacob, that ain't no whiskey glass," moaned Turk.

"It's one whiskey," Jacob said defensively.

"Go in the back and get the wanted poster off my desk and bring it out here to show him," ordered Turk.

"Do I get another whiskey?"

"I think you got enough whiskey," blurted Turk.

Jacob went to the little office, picked up the wanted poster and brought it out to the bar. He looked back and forth between the poster and Malone's face and nodded his head.

"That's his face on here," said Jacob. "Says he's wanted for one thousand dollars. That's a lot of money."

"Come around here and take his pistol and check him for any other weapons," Turk told Jacob. "And stay to one side of him so I don't shoot you too."

Jacob came around the bar and moved to one side of Malone. He removed the pistol from his holster and felt around his waist for a gun or knife.

"Nothing," said Jacob.

"Take his boots off," ordered Turk.

Jacob pulled Malone's right boot off his foot and Malone use his right foot to kick Jacob in the face. Jacob fell backward onto the saloon floor. Turk fired one barrel of the shotgun over Malone's head. The buckshot peppered the ceiling.

"I got one barrel left and it'll take your head clean off your shoulders at this distance," warned Turk.

Jacob got on his hands and knees. He took off the other boot and a long thin-bladed knife fell out of it when Jacob turned it over.

"Just what I thought," said Turk.

"Now what?" asked Malone.

"Get on your knees," ordered Turk.

A half hour and some leather straps later found Malone hog-tied and on his stomach on the floor of Turk's little office.

The door was locked and a man sat outside the door with a sawed-off shotgun.

Jacob looked at Turk.

"What do we do with him now?" Jacob asked.

"Now, I wire that town marshal over in Stratton to come and get him," declared Turk.

CHAPTER FIVE

United States Marshal Frank Reedy was sitting in his office, having a sandwich for lunch when he heard the delivery boy, Melvin, thudding along the boardwalk coming his way. He set the sandwich down and waited.

Melvin ran past his door and kept going. He stopped at the town marshal's open door to see John Bodine sweeping the floor of his office, looking bored. He walked in and handed the message to Bodine.

"Says it's important that you get this immediately," said Melvin, shoving his hand out, palm side up.

Bodine reached into his pocket and dropped a nickel into the boy's palm and it snapped shut.

"You still overcharging Frank?" he asked.

"Yeah, he never knows how much I'll charge him each time," said Melvin.

"Well, you keep it up, Melvin," grinned Bodine. "Keeps him on his toes."

"Oh, don't you worry," chuckled Melvin, "I'll keep it up for sure."

Bodine unfolded the paper and read the message from Turk in the village of Fulton. When he saw the name of Ned Malone, he grunted and grinned.

Melvin ran out and headed back to the telegraph operator's office, running past Reedy's office as he did. Reedy watched him run by and snorted. He finished his sandwich and stood up.

After putting his hat on, he walked out to see John Bodine coming out of his office with his saddlebags and a rifle. He headed for Bodine, who stopped on the porch and waited for him.

"Where are you off to?" Reedy asked.

Bodine showed him the message and he smiled when he saw the name.

"Well, about time someone caught that crazy killer," said Reedy. "He's escaped from two jails and once from the state penitentiary. Turk over in Fulton caught him?"

"Said he just wandered into his saloon this afternoon," said Bodine. "I'll stay the night there and bring him here tomorrow."

"Well, have some of that turkey when you get there," said Reedy. "That man sure knows how to cook them big birds."

"Oh yeah, I'll be eating me some of that turkey while I'm there," he said. "You can be sure of that."

"Well, I'll see ya when you get back tomorrow," said Reedy. "I told Melvin to keep you on your toes too."

"Thanks, John. I don't think he needs any help from you."

Bodine lowered his head and chuckled.

Reedy

"No, I suppose he doesn't," he said as he headed to the livery.

He got his horse saddled and walked him out of the livery. After climbing up in the saddle, he left Stratton, heading for the village of Fulton.

He arrived later in the afternoon and headed straight for Turk's Saloon. He dismounted and climbed the steps. As soon as he pushed through the batwings, Turk smiled widely.

"Marshal John Bodine," he said excitedly. "Thanks for comin' so quickly. We got us a small fortune layin' in my office in the back."

"Let's see the sumbitch," said Bodine as he sniffed the aroma coming from the kitchen.

Turk led the way and Bodine followed. He stopped in the kitchen to smell the turkey cooking.

Turk stopped and turned.

"There'll be plenty of time to eat, John," he said. "Take a look at who we got."

Bodine nodded and walked to the door going to the office as the man with the shotgun moved and Turk unlocked the door. Bodine saw the man hog-tied and on his stomach.

"Someone, untie me," grumbled Malone.

Bodine pulled a pocketknife from his front pocket and cut the leather strap holding Malone's hands and feet together. He let out a long sigh and rolled onto his back. He saw Bodine standing there, a sly smile on his lips.

"Well, if it ain't John Bodine," he said contemptuously.

"How the hell did you get yourself caught by some locals?" Bodine asked.

"I guess I let my guard down," he admitted. "Ain't come across a lawman or bounty hunter lookin' for me in over a year. Guess I got lazy, thinkin' no one was chasin' me anymore."

"You raped and murdered the wife of a state supreme court justice of the state of Texas," exclaimed Bodine. "Did you think they'd just forget something like that?"

"Well, I was hopin'," he said.

"I'll be taking you to Stratton in the morning and putting you in my jail until the town of Calico can send some men to transport you there. The judge wants to personally pull the lever on the gallows when they hang you."

"I didn't know she was the wife of a high court justice," he groused.

"Like that makes a difference?" asked Bodine. "Tell that to the judge. He'll pronounce you guilty within the first five minutes of your trial and sentence you to hang by the neck until dead."

Bodine turned around to Turk.

"Uh, speakin' of necks, do you have a few turkey necks cooked for me?"

"Yeah, I put 'em in the oven right after I sent that wire out to you," said Turk. "I know how much you like 'em."

"I surely do," said Bodine as he looked at the guard with the shotgun.

"Hog-tie him again and leave him on his stomach for the night," Bodine told him.

"Aw, c'mon," wailed Malone. "It's an uncomfortable position to sleep in."

"Tell that to Cassie Hood, who's in a cold casket six feet under Texas soil," said Bodine in a rancorous tone of voice. "Maybe she'll have some pity on your sorry ass, but not me."

The guard retied the cut strap, making it even more uncomfortable for Malone.

Bodine looked at Turk.

"Change these guards out every two hours so no one gets sleepy," he ordered.

Turk nodded his head.

"Not a problem," said Turk, "I already have four men sleeping now to do just that. He ain't goin' nowhere."

"Good," said Bodine. "Now, let's go and start with them turkey necks."

Bodine sat at a table and ate the necks and then had a hot turkey sandwich covered in a thick rich gravy.

Turk came over when he was finished and took his plate.

"Did you get your fill?" he asked.

"Yes, I did," Bodine said as he patted his stomach. "You should change the name of this place to Turkey Town."

"I might think on that a bit," said Turk. "Now, we are gonna get that one thousand in bounty money for catching Malone, right?"

"Yep, every bit of it," assured Bodine. "Whose name do I put down on the paperwork?"

"My name, and the town's name," he said. "We're all gonna

share it among the townsfolk, since we could all use a little help these days."

"I think that's a fine way of doing it, Turk," agreed Bodine.

"Would you like more coffee and maybe some dessert? I still have a piece of boysenberry cobbler left."

"Dang if you didn't talk me right into it," said Bodine. "And have the liveryman get my horse and Malone's horse ready to ride in the morning from in front of the saloon."

"I'll take care of it," said Turk.

Turk brought him the dessert and more coffee. After that, Bodine retired to one of the rooms upstairs for the night.

In the morning, after a hearty meal, Bodine opened the door to the little office to find Malone snoring lightly. Bodine tapped him with his boot and he jerked awake.

"Huh, what?" he stammered, as dribble slipped off his lips.

Bodine cut the leather strap binding his hands and feet together. Malone's legs slowly flattened out on the floor. He turned to the guard.

"Cut his hands loose," Bodine told him as he drew his gun and cocked it.

The guard cut the leather binding Malone's wrists together behind his back. Malone brought his hands around in front and rubbed his wrists to get the circulation going.

"Help him to his feet," said Bodine.

The guard put the shotgun on his seat and Malone rolled over onto his back. The guard reached down with one arm and helped Malone to his feet.

Reedy

Bodine grinned at Malone.

"Let's have an understanding, me and you. You're wanted dead or alive, and the judge in Calico wants to hang you himself, but I'll have no problem or hesitation bringing you in dead. Putting a bullet in your sorry ass would be no different than shootin' a snake."

Bodine looked at the guard again.

"Tie his wrists together in front," he ordered.

The guard tied his wrists together in front and Bodine waved the cocked pistol at Malone.

"Let's go," said Bodine. "Your horse is out front."

He marched Malone through the kitchen, through the saloon and out in front, where the two horses were waiting.

"Get up on your horse and don't try anything funny," cautioned Bodine.

Malone looked at the several men standing outside the saloon, all with rifles in their hands. He climbed up in the saddle and nodded toward the local men.

"Don't look like I'd make it far anyway," said Malone.

"Maybe twenty feet or so," guessed Bodine as he released the hammer on his pistol.

He holstered it and climbed up in the saddle. He slid out his rifle, levered a round into it and released the hammer.

"You ride in front of me," said Bodine. "East out of town to Stratton, where a nice clean jail cell awaits your arrival."

Malone sighed heavily and turned his horse out of town.

They rode along the trail for an hour or so when Bodine had the strange feeling he was being watched.

"Hold up," said Bodine.

Malone stopped his horse and turned in the saddle.

"What is it?" Malone asked.

"I dunno," muttered Bodine. "I just had an odd feeling for some reason."

"You lawmen are all the jumpy type," said Malone. "It's probably nothing."

"Yeah, you're probably right," agreed Bodine. "Get moving again."

Malone started his horse again. Bodine didn't see the slight smile forming on his evil lips.

CHAPTER SIX

Jess finished walking around the town of Alger and ended up in front of Gracie's Café. Before he walked inside, he looked at the big black-and-white paint horse in front of the saloon.

"That's new," he said to himself before entering the café.

He walked in and found Toby serving food to a table of two women. Jess sat at the same corner table as before.

Toby walked over to him.

"Gracie is making fried chicken today," he said. "It's really good."

"I'll take it," said Jess.

Toby disappeared in the kitchen and returned in a few minutes with a heaping platter of fried chicken and potatoes. He set it on the table, along with a cup of coffee. Jess looked at him.

"Toby, is there someone new over at the saloon?"

"Yeah, he rode in a few minutes ago. Why?"

"What does he look like?"

"Well, he's got a fancy holster and gun and he'd dressed kind of nice," he said. "He's got fancy snakeskin boots with spurs. Why?"

"Did he mention his name?"

"Nah, but I was only in there long enough to deliver chicken dinners to some of the customers."

"Thanks, Toby," he said.

"Do you want me to go find out who he is?"

"No, absolutely not, Toby," Jess told him.

The boy went to clean off a table after the people left. Jess took his time and enjoyed the fried chicken. After he finished eating, he left a five-dollar gold piece on the table. He donned his hat and stood up, looking at the window of the kitchen to see Gracie staring back at him.

"Did you like the chicken?"

"It was delicious," he told her.

He walked out and stood outside, looking at the black-and-white horse. Walking slowly toward it, he saw the letters L W carved into the leather on the side of the saddle.

"Lovell Wise, a good friend of Jim Fisk," said Jess to himself. "I wonder what he could want here, after I just killed his best friend?"

He sighed, slipped his hammer strap off and headed up the steps. As soon as he reached the batwings, he saw Lovell Wise watching him in the mirror. The hammer strap was already off his Colt Peacemaker.

"I've been expecting you," Wise said as he slowly turned at the bar.

Jess pushed through the batwings and stood there.

Wise glanced at the untethered pistol.

"I see you were expecting to see me too," he said.

"As soon as I saw the initials on your saddle outside, I put it together," admitted Jess.

"Join me for a drink?" asked Wise.

Jess slowly made his way to the bar. The local men moved out of the way as he did. The owner and barkeep, Eleby Shore, grabbed a bottle of good whiskey and poured a little into a small glass. He slid it to Jess, who caught it with his left hand.

Wise smiled slightly.

"Just so you know, I've paid the local undertaker to bury my good friend, Jim Fisk, in the local cemetery," he said.

"Well, you wasted your money," advised Jess. "His body is going to Wendell to be turned into the law there for the bounty on his head."

Wise took a sip of his whiskey and set the glass down on the bar.

"The first mistake you're making there is assuming you'll be able to take his body to Wendell," professed Wise. "The second mistake or assumption you're making is that you'll make it out of this saloon alive. After all, you killed my best friend."

Light murmuring was heard around the room.

"I think you're making a lot of assumptions that just might be wrong," said Jess.

"Ah, and there it is," said Wise. "The notion that you can't be beat. I've heard all the rumors about you. The devil owns your right hand. You can't be killed. The devil won't let you die, and all the other things men say about you. But you see, I think that's all the same stuff that comes out of a bull's ass… which is just manure."

The batwings swung open and the undertaker showed up with a shovel. He looked at Jess and then at Wise.

"Well, I was out at the cemetery diggin' a hole when I saw Mr. Williams come in here, so I'm just checking to see what I'm supposed to do with that man's corpse."

"Bury it in the cemetery," said Wise.

"Where is the body now?" Jess asked.

"On my wagon over in front of my parlor."

"Leave it there for now," Jess told him.

"And I said, bury him in the cemetery," pressed Wise.

The undertaker's shoulders slumped and he looked frustrated.

"Which one of you is more likely to shoot me if I don't listen to you?" he asked.

"I am," said Wise.

"He is," Jess said as the same time.

The undertaker huffed.

"Sorry, Mr. Williams, but I'm goin' back to diggin' that grave."

"That's fine," said Jess. "One of us is gonna need it soon anyway."

The undertaker shrugged his shoulders and walked out, heading for the cemetery again.

Wise smiled smartly at Jess.

"Well, I guess we finally agree on one thing," he said. "One of us will need that grave before long. But who will it be? What do you think?"

"I just need to know if you want the standard white cross or a granite headstone," Jess said, a slightly evil grin on his face. "Kind of hard to make that kind of decision once you're dead.

"And I might ask you the same thing," said Wise.

"It doesn't matter if I'm dead," explained Jess. "I'll never get to see it anyway."

"I see your point," said Wise.

He took another sip of his whiskey and set the glass down, before moving a foot away from the bar. Jess moved away from it also.

"You killed my best friend, Williams," said Wise. "And now, you gotta pay for it."

"Is this worth it?" inquired Jess. "Fisk is already dead. This can't bring him back and you know that."

"That's not the issue here," argued Wise. "Fisk saved my hide twice and I owe it to him to avenge his death. It doesn't have to make sense. It just has to happen."

"Well, if I can't talk you outta this, we might as well get to it," declared Jess as he put his hands into position by his pistol.

Wise lowered his right hand down to the butt of his Colt. He widened his stance and shifted his shoulders around.

"By the way, what was Fisk worth anyway?" Wise asked.

"Three hundred, not that I killed him for the money."

"Yeah, I heard you're a rich man."

"I do okay."

"Too bad you're not going to get to spend all that money," Wise said as he narrowed his eyes and tightened his lips.

Wise stood stone-still for a few moments. Then, he blinked and went for his Colt. He was feeling good when his thumb cocked the hammer all the way back as the cylinder cleared the top of the holster.

The feeling turned bad instantly as his brain registered two slugs piercing his chest, causing him to stumble back two baby steps. He grunted as he looked down at the two crimson-red spots on his shirt.

"I guess I'll be the one needin' that grave after all," were the last words he ever spoke on this side of the living.

He slumped sideways against the bar, bounced off it and landed on his side several feet from it, dead. His lips puffed air and it was the last breath that would ever leave his body. Jess walked over, replaced the spent shells in his pistol and holstered it.

He walked back to where his drink was on the bar. He took a sip and stood there, looking at the body, thinking about how fleeting life could be and marveling at the ridiculous reasons men would gamble their lives.

The undertaker came walking in, his shovel in his hands. He looked at the body and then at Jess.

"I guess that hole is for him now," he said. "You makin' a claim for his things?"

Reedy

Jess shook his head.

"No, you do whatever you want with 'em," said Jess. "Just make sure that Fisk's body is tied down to his horse in the morning."

"I'll take care of it," said the merchant of death. "And I never doubted you'd be the one left standing."

"Thanks," said Jess.

The undertaker hauled the body out and down to the cemetery. Jess finished his drink, went upstairs and fell off to sleep, wondering what he'd find in Wendell tomorrow.

CHAPTER SEVEN

John Bodine rode into Stratton late in the afternoon. Malone was riding in front of him.

"Head straight for the jail, Malone," Bodine ordered.

Malone reined up in front of the town jail. Bodine dismounted and walked over to Malone, his rifle still in his hands. Malone started to dismount, but he used his free foot to kick Bodine in the chest, knocking him to the ground.

Malone swung back up in the saddle and heeled his horse into a run, away from the jail. Just before he passed Reedy's office, Reedy came out and fired his rifle at Malone's head.

The slug passed through his hat and it flew off his head. Reedy then aimed his rifle directly at Malone, who skidded his horse to a halt.

"Damn, Frank," Malone scoffed. "You nearly took my head off."

"I missed on purpose, but only because the judge in Calico wants to hang you personally."

"I think I'd rather be shot than to hang by the neck in front of a bunch of onlookers I ain't never seen before."

"Should have considered that before you committed the crime."

"I told Bodine I didn't know who she was."

"I told you, that doesn't matter!" scolded Bodine.

Bodine walked to the other side of Malone's horse, grabbed Malone by the shirtsleeve and yanked him off his horse. He hit the ground hard, grunting loudly.

"Dang, Bodine, take it easy," he railed.

"I think it's time you took a nap," said Bodine as he rammed the butt of his rifle against Malone's forehead.

He passed out cold and lay still on the ground.

Reedy walked around the horse and smiled at Bodine.

"I hope you didn't kill him," he said. "The judge really wants to hang him."

"Nah, he's still breathing," said Bodine, as he waved for a few of the local men to come over.

"Pick his sorry ass up and carry him to my jail," said Bodine.

"I'll take care of the horses," offered Reedy.

"Thanks, Frank," he said.

Reedy grabbed the reins to Malone's horse and walked to where Bodine's was still standing in front of the jail.

Melvin showed up on the boardwalk.

"Did Marshal Bodine kill that man?" he asked.

Reedy shook his head.

"No, he'll wake up soon," he explained. "He just knocked him out."

"Were you really gonna kill him if he hadn't stopped?" inquired Melvin.

"Of course, I would have," he explained. "It's my sworn duty. He's a vicious killer and he's gonna hang once he's delivered to Calico, where he strangled a woman to death."

Reedy left out the rape part, thinking young Melvin didn't need to know about that.

"I guess I didn't realize how dangerous your job was before," admitted Melvin.

Reedy stuck his finger in one ear and scratched it as he looked at the boy.

"Does that mean I'm gonna get a break on delivery fees from now on?" he asked.

Melvin smiled slyly as he squinted his eyes.

"Nice try, Marshal," he said grinning. "Not a chance."

Melvin took off running along the boardwalk.

Reedy chuckled.

"Yeah, I didn't think so either," he said before heading to Bodine's office.

When he walked inside, Bodine was locking the heavy door going to the back cells. The two local men walked out, nodding at Reedy as they did.

Bodine sat behind his desk and Reedy plopped down in one of the chairs in front of it. Bodine took off his hat and hung it on a peg behind him.

"Thanks for your help, Frank, although I already had him in my sights."

"I figured that, but didn't want to take any chances," said Reedy. "Once you get him delivered to the judge in Calico, he'll be extremely grateful, and that's a good thing. It's handy to have a friend in such high places."

"You talkin' about the favor thing?"

"Yeah, just think about it," said Reedy. "You need a warrant that some other judges won't give you, you call on Judge Hood and he'll hand it to you, no questions asked."

"I reckon you're right," Bodine agreed.

"I know I'm right," said Reedy. "Jess did a favor for Senator Thibabough and look what happened. He brought in a rail spur and a bunch of rich people who bought properties out on the lake and invested in this town. How do you think you became the highest paid town marshal in the entire state of Texas?"

"Then, how come I don't have me a deputy?"

Reedy leaned forward on Bodine's desk.

"Well, because I'm here to back you up when you need it, but mostly, because you haven't asked for one."

"Maybe I'll talk to Mayor Fleming about that," said Bodine.

"He's only been in the position for a few months now, but I'm sure he'll be okay with it, especially if Henry Stratton approves, and I'm certain he will. I'll send the wire out to Judge John Hood about the capture of Ned Malone and then get back to my office."

"You taking another nap after all that excitement?" joked Bodine.

"No, I'm working on my file cabinet of wanted posters," he said.

"Frank, you must have the largest and most organized collection of wanted posters in the country, old and new."

"Yep, and they've come in handy a dozen times," said Frank.

He stood up and headed back to his office, where Melvin was standing and waiting for him with a slip of paper in his hand.

"Whatcha got for me, Melvin?"

"A message from Jess telling you he caught Jim Fisk and is taking his body to Wendell to turn into the law there."

Reedy took the slip of paper, unfolded it, and read the message.

"You need to send a response?"

"Not about this. He's just lettin' me know his location and what he's doing. I do need to send him a message though."

He went to his desk and jotted down a message to Jess, informing him of the capture of Ned Malone and letting him know he was locked in the jail in Stratton. He handed the message to Melvin.

"How much this time?"

"Nary a cent."

"What? Nothing at all?"

"Well, I saw you actually had to exert yourself today, stopping that killer and all, so I thought I'd give you a break on this one."

"Are you sure, Melvin?" he asked, a suspicious look on his face.

"Yeah, 'cause I can always charge you double on the next one," Melvin said as he took off running back to the office.

Reedy shook his head.

"Conniving little shit," he said and headed into his office.

He wrote a message to Judge Hood and headed to the telegraph office to get it sent out right away. Melvin wasn't sitting on his bench. The operator sent the message out and handed the message back to him.

Reedy took a nickel out of his front pocket and put it on the bench for Melvin. The operator chuckled and Reedy looked over at him.

"What's so funny?" Reedy asked.

"Well, knowing Melvin the way I do, he might just leave an invoice on that bench for you saying you owe him another nickel," he said.

"Yeah, well, keep laughing, 'cause he might just have your job one day," said Reedy.

The smile disappeared from the operator's face.

***

Wendell was an average-sized town with plenty of homes and businesses located on the main street and the two side streets to the north and to the south. Some homes were scattered around the streets in no particular order.

Recently, the town residents had elected a mayor and two councilmembers to run the town. Shortly thereafter, it was decided that the mayor would oversee the appointment of a town marshal.

The marshal, Ryder Martin, was young and skinny and wore a Colt on his right hip. He was vastly inexperienced, but he was the nephew of the mayor and the only one who would accept the job at fifty dollars a month.

Martin was sitting in a rocking chair outside the newly built town jail in the early afternoon when he saw a man riding into town with a packhorse next to him and another horse behind it with a dead body tied down to it.

He saw the shotgun handle sticking over the man's right shoulder, but he still didn't know who the man was. He seemed to be heading his way, so he stood up and waited.

Jess reined up in front of Martin and slid from the saddle. He walked up the steps and shook hands with the marshal.

"I heard they hired on a new marshal," said Jess.

"Yeah, for fifty a month," he said. "Who you got on that horse back there?"

Jess removed the wanted poster on Jim Fisk and handed it to him.

He looked it over and sighed.

"I gotta admit, I've never handled one of these before," he said. "I don't even know if we have the proper paperwork in my new office."

"Do you know the county sheriff?" Jess asked.

"Yeah."

"Well, he'll have the proper forms to give you to get started," said Jess. "I can give you my banker's information and when you get the papers filed, send my money to him. You keep ten percent for your troubles."

Martin still looked confused and he swiveled his head to the left to see the mayor walking toward them. He was a large-framed man with black trousers, a white shirt, and a white Stetson.

"Oh, here comes our new mayor," said Martin. "Maybe he can help."

"My, my, my," drawled the mayor. "Jess Williams, in the flesh."

"You know me?" Jess asked him.

"I surely do," he said as he stuck his hand out to shake. "I'm Jubal Bower and I was recently elected to the position of mayor of Wendell. I've read all sorts of books and articles about you."

Bower turned to the marshal.

"Do you know that this man has brought in more wanted men than all the other bounty hunters combined west of the Mississippi?"

"Uh...no, I didn't," admitted Martin.

"Well, I'll take care of the payment for whoever he has back there and settle it all later, after we get things set right in your office with the proper paperwork and all," said the mayor.

"Yes, sir," said Martin.

"Come to the city office tomorrow morning and I'll have the money ready," Bower told the marshal. "Who did he bring in and how much is he worth?"

Martin looked at the wanted poster again.

"Jim Fisk. He's worth three hundred dollars," he told the mayor.

"Come see me in the morning," said Bower as he headed along the boardwalk toward the city offices.

Martin turned to Jess.

"Well, that was unusual, I think," said Martin.

"Yeah, that was very unusual for a mayor," admitted Jess.

"Uh, do I still get ten percent?"

"I'll tell you what," said Jess. "Let's make it twenty percent."

"Really?"

"Yeah."

"Thanks," he said excitedly. "The hotel down the street has nice rooms and the saloon on Main Street has good food."

"I'm gonna take care of my horses and get a room," he said.

"I'll meet you for breakfast in the saloon in the morning," said Martin.

"See ya then."

He untied the horse with Fisk's corpse and handed it to the marshal. Then he headed for the livery.

CHAPTER EIGHT

Texas State Supreme Court Justice John Hood sat in his large house in Calico, Texas, looking at the photograph of him and his dearly departed wife, Cassie, on the day they were married.

They had been happily married for ten years, until the outlaw, Ned Malone, took all that away from them.

Malone had broken into their house late at night, robbed them of the cash they had in the house, and proceeded to rape and then strangle Cassie to death.

It had been almost two years now since the incident, and he still spent his mornings sipping coffee and looking at the photo that he left on the kitchen table.

He was interrupted by a knock at the door. He got up, walked to the front door and peered through the curtains. It was the telegraph operator. He opened the door and sighed, thinking he had been assigned a new case.

"What is it?" he asked.

"It's good news," said the operator as he handed the message to him. "They caught the man who murdered Cassie."

The judge immediately became excited.

"How? Who? Where? When?"

"Some men in the village of Fulton caught him and turned him over to Marshal John Bodine in Stratton. He's in the jail there right now."

Hood read the message and when he finished, he looked up at the operator.

"Go and fetch Marshal Clinton and tell him to report to me immediately," ordered Hood.

"Yes, sir, your honor," he said.

He took off running toward the main street where the jail was. Hood closed the door and went back to the table and sat down. He picked up the photo and kissed it gently.

"I know it won't bring you back, my love, but at least the man who took you from me will pay dearly for what he did to you. I promise."

He sobbed quietly at the table, remembering all the happy days with his wife. Picnics out by the large oak tree north of town. Fishing in the river behind their home. Nightly walks whenever he wasn't traveling to dispense justice.

Hearing another knock on his door, he looked up from the photo.

"Come in," he said loudly.

Town Marshal Randy Clinton opened the door and walked through the vestibule and then into the kitchen. He was a short

Reedy

wiry man with a handlebar mustache that was neatly trimmed and curled up at the end.

His gun rode in his holster low on his right leg. He removed his brown bowler hat and held it against his chest.

"I heard the good news, your honor," he said. "I reckon you want me to send some men to haul his miserable ass here to be hung?"

"Yes, send your deputy and deputize another man to go with him to Stratton to get him," he said without looking up from the photo.

"Yes, sir, I'll send Deputy Harry Tweed and I'll deputize Alvie Dearman to go with him."

"Tell them to leave first thing in the morning."

"I'll make certain of it," said the marshal.

"Oh, and send a message to Marshal John Bodine, saying that Malone is not to be let out of the cell for any reason," said Hood. "Not to relieve himself or be tended to by a doctor. Tell him that's an order directly from me, and if he violates it, I'll have his hide and his badge."

Clinton turned and walked out, heading for the jail. When he arrived, his deputy, Harry Tweed, was sitting behind his desk in the far corner.

He looked up at Clinton.

"Let me guess," he said, "I'm heading to Stratton tomorrow morning?"

"Yeah, go find Alvie and bring him in here so I can deputize him."

"All right, I'll go get him now," he said, donning his hat and standing up.

He headed straight for the blacksmith shop, where Alvie Dearman worked. When he arrived, he found him pounding on a horseshoe on a metal anvil. He stopped when he saw Tweed approaching.

"What do you need?" Dearman asked.

"Marshal Clinton wants you over at the office, pronto," said Tweed.

"Can I finish this shoe first?"

"It's for the judge."

"Oh, okay," he said as he left the shoe on the anvil, put the hammer on the workbench and removed his heavy leather apron.

He followed Tweed to the jail and walked in behind him.

Marshal Clinton was polishing a deputy's badge and looked up at Dearman.

"Put your right hand up," he said.

Dearman's shoulders slumped and he sighed.

"Why me again?" he moaned.

"Because you're the only one in town with any law experience," answered Clinton.

"I'm regrettin' that more and more each day. What is it this time?"

"The marshal over in Stratton is holding the man who killed Cassie Hood," explained Clinton. "I need you to go with Tweed here and bring him here to be hung by the judge."

"When do we leave?"

"First thing tomorrow morning," said Clinton.

Dearman raised his right hand. Clinton swore him in and handed him the badge.

He pinned it on his shirt and sighed.

"There was a day I enjoyed wearing one of these, but those days are gone," he sighed. "I'll get my gear ready for the morning. Got a horse for me?"

"Yep, he's at the livery now," said Clinton. "Liveryman will show you which one."

"All right, anything for the judge," said Dearman.

"Good, now, I gotta go send a message to John Bodine in Stratton," said Clinton.

Dearman left and Tweed sat down behind his desk. Clinton headed to the telegraph operator's office.

The operator sent the message out and looked up at Clinton when he was finished.

"I'm sure glad they caught that sumbitch," he said.

Clinton nodded.

"Maybe the judge will finally get a little peace after he pulls that lever," he declared.

***

Back in Stratton, Frank Reedy was coming out of the Stratton Hotel, after talking to Henry Stratton regarding the hiring of a deputy for John Bodine. He saw Melvin running along the boardwalk, bypassing his office, and heading for Bodine's.

Reedy stepped off the boardwalk and headed for Bodine's office.

Melvin ran out before he reached it and he waved at Reedy.

"Thanks for the nickel," said Melvin without looking over at him.

Reedy walked into Bodine's office when he was reading the message from the marshal of Calico. He put it down on his desk and looked at Reedy.

"Judge Hood has ordered me to keep Malone behind bars at all times," he explained. "No privy breaks, and if he needs to see a doctor, he's to be put in shackles and kept in the cell while the doctor tends to his needs."

"Well, get some buckets and don't feed him all that much," advised Reedy.

"To be honest, I agree with the judge," said Bodine. "He's escaped too many times already. He ain't getting away from me, no way."

"If you need anything from me, just holler," said Reedy.

"What? Your hearing gettin' worse?"

"Don't get smart with me," snapped Reedy.

Bodine chuckled.

"I'm gonna post a night guard in the jail."

"Good. I talked to Henry about a deputy for you and he's in agreement. He'll talk to the mayor for you."

"Thanks, Frank."

Reedy

Reedy stood and returned to his office. Bodine walked out and headed to the Stratton Hotel to see if Henry could spare one of his personal guards to cover the night shift at the jail.

CHAPTER NINE

After stabling his horses in the livery in Wendell, Jess headed to the town's hotel. When he walked in, a young man was standing at the front desk.

"I heard there was a famous bounty hunter in town," he said. "You need a room for the night?"

"Yeah, your best room," said Jess.

The man frowned.

"Oh, sorry, but a famous gunslinger already rented the only nice suite we have."

"Really? Who?"

The man looked at the register and then spun it around for Jess to see.

"His name is Carl Savage. He's quite famous out East," he said as he tapped on the name. "He checked in early this morning."

"Hmm, never heard of this man before," said Jess. "Give me your next best room."

"It's for a family and has two double beds in it. It'll cost you six dollars a night."

"That's fine."

Jess paid him and he gave him the key. A young woman came walking down the steps with a bucket and a brush.

"Oh, this is my wife Gloria. She does most of the housekeeping in the hotel," he said.

She smiled at Jess.

"If you need anything, just ask me or Devin here," she said.

"The man from out East who checked in this morning? Is he still in his room?"

"No, I just tidied up his room a few minutes ago," she said.

"Yeah, he left right after he checked in this morning," added Devin.

"Did he say where he was going?"

"No, and I didn't ask," said Devin.

"Thanks," said Jess as he headed up the steps.

Gloria looked at Devin.

"Why do you think he asked about Mr. Savage?"

"Well, I'm not sure, but I think we should stay out of it, whatever it is."

"I suppose so," she said as she headed to the storage room to get more clean bedding for another room.

Jess put his rifle and saddlebags in his room and locked the door when he left. He headed out of the hotel and straight to the marshal's office.

Ryder Martin was in his rocking chair outside on the boardwalk in front.

"We don't have your bounty money yet, Mr. Williams," he said.

"I'm not here about that," he said as he reached him. "What do you know about the man who checked into the hotel early this morning?"

"Not much," he admitted. "He checked in and left about fifteen minutes later on his horse."

"Did you talk to him or ask him what he was doing in town?"

He shook his head.

"Nah, I figured him for a gunslinger or lawman, although he didn't have a badge of any sorts."

"How long have you been on this job?"

"Two weeks now."

"Let me give you some advice, Marshal. When someone new rides into your town, you stop them and ask them who they are and why they're here. That puts them on notice that you're watching them."

"Ain't that being kind of nosy?"

Jess smiled and sighed.

"It's your duty and obligation to be nosy. This is your town. Whenever something bad happens, it's your problem to clean up. Best you know who you're dealing with right away."

"How do you know so much about the law business?"

Jess pulled his Deputy United States Marshal badge out of his front pocket and showed it to him.

"I get called on special assignments from the Federal Marshals from time to time. And I've been in the business of bounty hunting for some time now. I don't do it part-time; I do this almost every day, so I've learned a lot over the years."

"You're a federal marshal?"

"Yeah."

"Shouldn't we tell the mayor about that?"

"No, he doesn't need to know."

"Okay," Martin said as he looked to the right.

Jess swiveled his head at the same time to see a well-dressed man walking his horse into town. As soon as the man saw Jess talking with the marshal, he stopped his horse.

Carl Savage sat tall in the saddle. He was a good-looking man, clean shaven, and had a fancy silver engraved Colt in his black holster.

He took a thin cheroot from his front pocket, put it between his lips and struck a lucifer to life with his left thumbnail. He lit the smoke and took in a long drag from it, letting the smoke filter from his nostrils.

Throwing the match on the ground, he heeled his horse forward again toward Jess and the marshal. When he reached them, he removed the smoke from his lips and held it down by his left leg.

"Are you who I think you are?" he asked.

Jess smiled slightly.

"Depends on who you think I am."

"I came out West in search of the infamous bounty hunter and mankiller, Jess Williams. He's supposed to have a unique pistol on his right leg and a sawed-off shotgun in a back sling. You look like you might fit the description."

"And if I am him, what do you want with him?"

"I can't find anyone left to challenge in the East, so I came out here, hoping to find a challenge worthy of my right hand. Are you worthy?"

"Well, the problem with that question is that to find out the answer, one of us will die."

"I understand that, but I need to know."

"I'm the man you're looking for, if that helps."

"So, you are Jess Williams."

"Yep."

"Well then, I seem to be at a crossroad in my life," he said. "Do I challenge you to answer my quest, or not."

"That's a big decision to make, especially when your life depends on the outcome."

"Yes, I suppose it is," he said matter-of-factly. "Now that I've found you and know what you look like, I suppose I've got some serious thinking to do."

"It would seem so," agreed Jess.

Savage stuck the cheroot back between his lips, tipped his hat at Jess and headed for the livery.

Marshal Martin let out a long breath.

"Wow, that was sumthin'," he said.

"It happens a lot."

"Really?" he asked.

"Yep."

"Do you think he'll challenge you?"

"He hasn't made up his mind yet."

"How do you know?"

"True and false words can come out of a man's mouth, but the eyes...they never lie," explained Jess.

"So, what if he decides to go through with it?"

"I've never run from a fight yet, and I'm not about to start now."

"Should I go tell the mayor about this?"

"Doesn't matter. Whatever is gonna happen is gonna happen, and the only ones who can change that are him or me."

"Well then, I should tell the mayor about it," said the marshal.

"I'm going to the saloon to see what's for supper later and then to the telegraph office to send out a wire to someone."

Jess went to the saloon, which was call Pirate's Cove Saloon. When he walked in, the man behind the bar wore a black patch over one eye.

Jess walked up to him and narrowed his eyes at the patch.

"You blind in that eye?" Jess asked.

"Nah, it's just for looks, you know, Pirate's Cove and all," he said as he lifted the patch to reveal a perfectly good eye.

"Interesting," he said. "So, what's for supper later?"

"Corned beef and cabbage," he said. "Maybe another hour or so."

"I'll be back later," said Jess.

He headed out to the telegraph office, his eyes following the wires to tell him where it was. When he walked in, the operator looked up at him.

"I've got a message addressed to you from a Frank Reedy," he said as he handed him the message.

Jess read it and grunted.

"Seems my friends caught Ned Malone," said Jess.

"The man who murdered that state supreme court judge's wife?"

"Yep."

Jess wrote down a message to Reedy, informing him of Carl Savage and letting Reedy know he was available if he needed any help regarding Malone.

The operator sent it out and Jess left, heading for the saloon again. As soon as he walked in, the place went eerily silent, a tension filling the air.

He looked over at a corner table where Savage sat alone, sipping some fine whiskey. He knew Jess had walked in, but he didn't even look at him. Jess walked up to the bar and the barkeep walked over to him.

"Are you and him gonna have a lead party later?" he asked Jess, who craned his neck over his shoulder to see Savage, still not paying him any attention.

"He hasn't made up his mind yet," said Jess as he looked at the barkeep again. "So, is supper ready yet?"

"That's what you're worried about, supper?"

"A man's still gotta eat, gunfight or not."

CHAPTER TEN

Vic Walker rode back into the camp where Tad waited for his return. Tad had been abandoned as a young child and never knew his last name, so he just went by Tad. They were camped about five miles outside of Stratton, Texas.

Walker was an ugly man by any standards. He wore a heavy beard and mustache to hide his ugliness, but it didn't help that much.

His forehead stuck out farther than normal and he had one lazy eye that seem to wander. He was a man of average size and had dark greasy-looking hair that seldom got washed. He wore a beat-up pistol on his right leg. Even his hat had seen better days.

Tad, who was older and skinny, with beady eyes and a bald patch on the top of his head, stood by the fire and frowned at Walker.

"What the hell took you so long?" he asked.

Walker dismounted, loosened the cinch strap on his horse and walked to the fire.

"I have to be extra careful not to be noticed," said Walker. "In case your memory is slipping, there's a town marshal in Stratton as well as United States Marshal Frank Reedy."

"Well, what'd you find out?"

"They have Malone in the jail," he answered. "And they ain't lettin' him out for privy breaks or anything."

"Did you see him?" asked Tad.

"No, I just talked to a few of the locals in one of the smaller saloons at the outer edge of town. Supposedly, the town of Calico is sending two deputies to come and transport our boss to Calico, where the judge is supposed to pull the lever to hang him personally."

"We can't let them get Malone to that town," advised Tad. "Once they have him there, it'll be impossible to break him out."

"Well, we can't break him out of that jail in Stratton either," declared Walker. "Bodine is not one to mess with and Frank Reedy is one tough old cuss. I ain't tangling with either of 'em. Plus, Henry Stratton has at least four professional hired guards working for him."

"We have to wait for Willie to show up yet," said Tad. "That way, we'll have at least three men. I figure we should hit them when they take Malone out of the jail and transport him to Calico."

Walker went to his horse and pulled out a whiskey bottle from his saddlebags. He walked back to the fire and they both sat down. Walker pulled out the cork, took a swig and handed it to Tad. He took a swig and looked like he was thinking about something.

"What's on your mind, Tad?"

He looked up at Walker.

"What if we wait along the trail from Calico and kill the two deputies heading to Stratton to pick up Malone?"

"Well, they're leaving Calico in the morning, so we'd have to leave in the morning too and ride along the trail toward them," suggested Walker. "We could surprise them straight on or find a spot where we could ambush them. That would slow things down a mite and maybe Willie can reach us before they figure out something else."

"Okay then, we leave first thing in the morning," said Tad.

***

Jess stood at the bar, eating supper and watching Carl Savage in the mirror. Jess had removed his hammer strap as a precaution, but he sensed that Savage would not resort to any underhanded tactics.

Savage was a professional shootist, with a reputation that he had obviously built up over the years. Pulling a gun on someone without proper warning would destroy his reputation in one fell swoop.

Jess didn't know much at all about Savage. He hoped that Reedy would give him some insight on the man, but it would probably come too late. If Savage was going to make his play, it would most likely be tonight.

He finished eating and had the barkeep bring him a cup of coffee. As he sipped his coffee, he saw that Savage was deep in thought, considering his odds against the man he knew little about, except what he had read or heard from friends and acquaintances out East.

Savage sat there, nursing his drink, calculating his odds. He had heard about the speed of Jess's right hand, but he had never witnessed it himself. But then again, if he knew a man's hand speed on the draw and knew for certain he could beat him, what would be the challenge?

Slowly, he stood up, picked up his drink and made his way to the bar. The other two men standing at the bar quickly moved away and over to a table. Savage set his drink down and looked at the barkeep.

"Did you go blind in one eye?" he asked.

"No, I just wear it for the whole idea of this being Pirate's Cove," he said as he moved the eyepatch to show a perfectly fine eye.

"Oh, okay then," he said. "Have you ever seen a real pirate?"

"No, but when I lived in the southernmost part of Florida, there was always talk of pirates roaming the seas around the area. Some of the local taverns had pictures of pirate ships and pirates. It always struck my fancy, so when I moved out here, I named the place Pirate's Cove and started wearing the eye patch."

"Maybe I'll have to go down there some day," said Savage.

The barkeep looked at Jess and grunted before turning back to Savage.

"Maybe. Maybe not," was all he said.

"Oh, so you don't think I should challenge Jess Williams?"

"Well, maybe you should go visit Florida first," inferred the barkeep.

"You didn't answer my question."

"If you want my honest opinion, no, you shouldn't challenge him."

"Why do you say that?"

"Men who live and die by the gun are different out here in the West," the barkeep explained. "You might be the best in the East, but out here in the West, men are used to dying from a chunk of lead. See, that man there, Jess Williams? If you brace him, he won't be thinking about dying or losing, he'll only be thinking about his reaction time. Watching your every move. Reading your eyes. Now, you on the other hand, will be wondering and worrying about losing and dying. He won't give none of that one tiny bit of a thought. That's the advantage he'll have over you. He'll just wait for the right moment, shuck that gun out and kill ya. You've been sitting over there stewing about your decision. He ain't given that one second of his time. When he walked up to the bar earlier? Do you want to know what he was thinkin' about?"

"No, what?" asked Savage.

"He wanted to know if supper was ready yet," said the barkeep.

"Really?"

"Yeah."

Savage sighed and tapped his glass.

"Touch more of that good whiskey," he said.

"Sure," said the barkeep.

He poured a little more whiskey into the glass and moved to the far end of the bar. Savage pondered about what the barkeep said. But he had traveled all this way for just this moment.

Why should he walk away now, when he had the biggest challenge of his life standing fifteen feet away from him? He moved closer to Jess, sliding his glass along the bar as he did.

Jess finally turned to him.

"Still thinking about it?" he asked.

"Yeah," said Savage. "You don't get nervous about this?"

"Nope."

"Not afraid of dying?"

"I should have been dead a dozen times already," professed Jess. "I don't give it any thought. When the devil thinks I'm ready, he'll take me. Until then, I'll just keep hunting the worst of men and sending them his way."

"And if I challenge you and beat you?"

"Then this is where I die," he said, shrugging his shoulders indifferently. "I'm gonna die someday, somewhere, and somehow. We all will."

"Fascinating," said Savage. "Out East, I've seen men sweat during a gunfight with me. One man even pissed himself. Another dropped his gun belt and ran for the hills. Never even came back for his horse. But you, you don't seem a bit worried."

"Worry will only get you killed," said Jess. "So, what have you decided?"

Savage took another sip of his whiskey and stood there, eyeballing Jess.

"I think I'm going to wait a while yet," he said. "I'm gonna follow you around for a bit and see. I've never met a man with an outlook quite like yours."

"Well, I'm fairly certain you're not a back shooter or someone who would sneak up on a man."

"No, if I were to challenge you, it'd be fair and straightforward. No tricks, no cheating and certainly, no back shooting."

"I believe you."

"Well, I'm going back to my table to have supper," said Savage.

Jess finished his drink, walked out and headed for the hotel. When he stepped inside, Devin was working the counter and his wife was sitting on a sofa in the lobby.

"Ma'am," said Jess as he walked by her.

"I've turned down your bed for you, Mr. Williams," she said.

He stopped and turned to her, smiling.

"That's very nice of you to do so, but I'd rather no one goes into my room when I'm out."

"Oh, I'm sorry," she said.

"Don't be," he told her. "I forgot to mention it, and thank you."

He headed up the steps to his room. Devin looked at his wife, shrugging his shoulders. Jess went into his room and checked his rifle to make sure it was fully loaded. Then he undressed and crawled into the bed.

He slowly fell off to sleep, wondering about Carl Savage and what he was eventually going to do. Then, he thought about the two wanted posters he had in his pocket, wondering which one he should go after first.

CHAPTER ELEVEN

Deputy Marshals Harry Tweed and Alvie Dearman found themselves in the livery in Calico, getting their horses ready to make the trip to Stratton to pick up the outlaw, Ned Malone.

Tweed had packed manacles in his saddlebags to use on Malone. There was no way he was going to let the outlaw escape his custody. He turned to Dearman.

"Listen, once we take custody of Malone, we ain't losing him or the judge will have our hide," explained Tweed. "I want you to always have your rifle at the ready. If he somehow makes a run for it with his horse, shoot the horse first."

"You want me to shoot his horse?"

"I don't like the idea either, but a horse is a bigger target and once the horse is down, he can't outrun a bullet on foot."

"You're really serious about it, ain't ya?"

"I am," he said. "It's only a one-day ride to Stratton, but it'll probably take two days to get back from there hauling a prisoner."

"All right, you're the boss so I'll do what you say," agreed Dearman.

They walked their horses out of the livery and mounted up. Judge Hood was standing outside his house. They rode to the front of it and stopped.

"You men have your orders," barked the judge. "Men will start building the gallows today."

"We'll bring him to you, Judge," said Tweed. "I promise."

"Don't let him escape again," pressed Hood. "He's a cagey bastard and has escaped custody more than once."

"Not with me, Judge," Tweed said confidently.

"All right then, on your way," he said.

Tweed and Dearman headed out of town.

Dearman looked over at Tweed.

"You shouldn't make promises you might not be able to keep," he said.

Tweed ignored him and kept riding, picking up the pace. Dearman shook his head, but said nothing more about the matter.

***

Jess was eating his breakfast in the Pirate's Cove Saloon in Wendell, when Marshal Ryder Martin walked in carrying an envelope. Martin sat down across from him and slid the envelope across the table.

"Did you take your share out of it?" Jess asked.

"Yeah, I hope you don't mind."

"No, not at all."

Martin glanced over at Carl Savage at a table, eating. He looked back at Jess.

"He hasn't made a challenge yet?" asked Martin.

"No, he wants to study me first."

"Really?"

"Yeah, he seems to be a little impressed with how we do things out here in the West."

"Aren't you leaving today?"

"Yeah."

"So, what? He's gonna follow you around?"

"I reckon."

"Ain't that dangerous? A gunslinger following you around wherever you go?"

"It is…for him."

"Oh. So, where are you off to next?"

"I've got a man who's supposedly staying in Galantine, Texas. His name is Myer Bollington and he's wanted for two hundred. Thought I'd take a ride there and see if he's still hanging around."

"Well, best of luck to you," said Martin.

"Thanks, although, I'm not sure how much luck has to do with any of it."

Jess finished eating and went to the hotel. He checked out, retrieved his things and headed for the livery. After getting his horses ready, he walked them out of the livery. He swung up in the saddle and took out the wanted poster on Myer Bollington.

He shook his head as he read the list of offenses and put the poster back into his pocket. He nudged Gray into a walk toward the end of the main street. As he passed the saloon, Savage was standing on the porch, watching him with interest.

He headed out along a trail that would lead him to the town of Galantine, knowing it would take him two days to reach it. He stopped several times to watch his back trail. Even though he didn't see Savage, he knew he was there, he could feel it.

When it got closer to the end of the day, he started looking for a good place to camp. He found it way off the trail in some heavy scrub oak. He strung his cans and cooked a simple meal.

When he finished eating, he walked out to the main trail with his spyglass and peered through it. He saw a fire right off the trail to one side. Lowering the spyglass, he shook his head.

"It's a miracle he hasn't been waylaid yet."

He went back to his camp and doused the fire with some sand. Crawling into his bedroll, he fell off to sleep.

At the camp where Savage was, dawn was just making its first appearance. He slowly got out of his bedroll and threw more branches on the glowing embers to get a fire going again.

He was on his knees, using his hat to fan the embers, when suddenly, he heard a hammer being pulled back. He froze and slowly raised his hands.

"You're gonna get yourself killed out here, camping like this," advised Jess.

Savage looked over at him. He was on his knees behind some bushes, his rifle aimed straight at Savage. Jess released the hammer and slowly stood up.

"Jeez, you scared the shit out of me," Savage said, letting out a long sigh of relief.

"Yeah, well, if it was someone else, you might be dead right now. You can't make camp twenty feet off the edge of a main trail. You need to go at least a few hundred yards off to one side of it and find a place with some cover. And you kick the fire out before dark so you can't be spotted by ambushers and outlaws."

"I never had to do that out East," he said.

"Well, you're not out East anymore. The farther you go west, the less civilized men are. They'll kill you just for the food on your fire and think nothing of it."

Savage stood up.

"Well then, why don't we travel together?"

"I'm not protecting some tenderfoot from out East."

"I'm not a tenderfoot. I'm a professional shootist, maybe just as good as you."

"Maybe you are at drawing that hog leg on your hip, but that's only one of a thousand ways to die out here in the West. They'll kill you for that money you have in your saddlebags."

"How do you know about that money?"

"I looked in them while you were snoring loud enough to alert anyone within a quarter-mile from here. You've got to learn to sleep lightly out on the trail or make sure you're able to reach the next town before dark and get a room."

"Well, I guess I'm not used to the customs out this far west."

"You'd better learn fast before someone shoots you in your sleep."

"So, why didn't you kill me when you had the chance?"

"Because I'm not a cold-blooded killer," explained Jess. "The only time you'll be a threat to me is when you're standing in front of me with your hammer strap off and your right hand down by the butt of your pistol. Not sleeping in a bedroll twenty feet off the main trail."

"I suppose you've proven that. I'll heed your suggestions."

"It might keep you alive a little longer."

"Well then, would you like to join me for breakfast?"

"No thanks," he said. "I'll be reaching the town of Galantine late in the afternoon. If you're going to follow me, check your map of the area."

"I don't have a map," admitted Savage.

Jess sighed heavily.

"When you reach Galantine, buy one," he said as he turned and headed for his camp.

Savage rubbed the back of his neck.

Jess reached his camp and cooked a quick meal. After that, he broke camp and headed along the main trail again, wondering if Savage would live long enough to decide whether to challenge him.

CHAPTER TWELVE

Deputy Marshals Harry Tweed and Alvie Dearman rode along the trail to Stratton. Around the noon hour, they stopped to have a quick lunch, consisting of beef jerky, biscuits and a can of peaches each.

Dearman was sitting on a huge rock and Tweed was leaning against his horse. They didn't see the wolfish eyes of the two men back in the small copse of young trees.

Vic Walker was aiming at Dearman and Tad had his sights on Tweed.

Walker kept his cheek on the buttstock of his rifle.

"We shoot on three," he said.

Tad nodded and kept his sights on Tweed.

Walker began counting.

"One...two...three."

Both men fired. Dearman took the slug to his back, severing his spine, killing him instantly. Walker's slug missed Tweed by an inch. Tweed reacted instantly, swinging up on his horse and getting ready to heel him into a dead run.

The moment his heels slammed the flanks of his horse, two slugs slammed into him. His horse took off, but he fell off the back of it and hit the ground hard on his head, snapping his neck in the process.

Walker and Tad walked out of the trees and over to the bodies. They took what money they had on them and dragged them thirty feet off the trail.

"Well, that ought to buy our boss an extra day or two," reasoned Walker.

"I believe you're right," agreed Tad. "Let's get back to our camp by Stratton and wait for Willie to show up."

The two walked back to their horses, climbed up in the saddle and headed out along the trail back to their camp.

***

It was late in the day when Reedy walked into Bodine's office. He sat down across the desk and set his hat on it.

"I haven't seen those two deputies in town yet," said Reedy. "Judge Hood wired me and said they had left early this morning."

"It's an easy day's ride here from Calico," said Bodine. "Maybe one of their horses threw a shoe or something happened to slow them down."

"Yeah, well, when it comes to Malone, I don't trust anything," said Reedy. "He's got friends out there, which is how he's escaped before. If they don't show up tonight, I'll ride out tomorrow looking for them."

Reedy

"You want me to go with you?"

"No, you stay here and make sure Malone stays in that jail."

"I suppose you're right," said Bodine as he looked at the clock on the wall. "They still could show up. There are still a few hours of daylight left."

"Just the same, I'm getting my horse ready for tomorrow, just in case," said Reedy as he stood up and donned his hat.

"All right," said Bodine.

"If they don't show up after dark, I'll wire Judge Hood to let him know," said Reedy.

***

Jess finally reached the town of Galantine, Texas, later in the afternoon. The town seemed to be a quiet and peaceful place. Seeing the late time of day, he headed for the livery first.

Deciding he'd stay the night whether Bollington was there or not, he rode to the front of the livery. A young man walked out.

"Welcome to Galantine, Mister," he said.

Jess slid from the saddle, walked his two horses inside and handed him the reins.

"Give 'em a good brush down and feed 'em your best," Jess told him as he handed him a five-dollar gold piece.

He looked at the coin and chuckled.

"How long you staying, mister?"

"Just the night, hopefully."

"Well, this is way too much money for one night."

"Well then, I guess the rest of it is for you treating my horses like they were your own."

"Thanks, mister," he said excitedly as an older man walked out from the back.

"What's goin' on out here?" he said as he looked Jess over.

He saw the shotgun handle sticking up over his right shoulder, the gun on his right thigh and the Colt stuck into the front of his holster. He noticed the four shotgun shells, stuffed into specially sewn-in pockets, two on each side of his stomach, above his gun belt.

"You must be either a lawman, shotgun rider for a stage or a bounty hunter," guessed the man.

"The last one," said Jess as he produced the wanted poster on Myer Bollington and showed it to him.

"Yeah, he was here for a day, but left two days ago," he said as he looked at the face on the poster.

"Did you see which way he rode out of town?"

"No, didn't pay any attention. He seemed like a right nice fella though. Even helped one of the women in town when she tripped on a loose board by the general store. Helped her up, picked up all her groceries and carried them home for her."

Jess put the wanted poster back into his pocket and pursed his lips.

"Trust me, he's a cold-blooded killer for sure," he said. "Who is the marshal in town?"

"Oh, that'd be Gill Lemon," he said. "He owns the Galantine Hotel with his wife, Gabby. She runs the place for him."

"Do you know where the marshal is now?"

"Usually in his office over at the jail," said the man.

"Thanks," said Jess as he took his rifle and saddlebags.

He walked out and headed to the jail, where he found the marshal sitting behind his desk, reading a two-day-old crumpled newspaper. He looked up at Jess when he walked in and smiled.

"What is Jess Williams doing in my neck of the woods?" he asked as he stood up and extended his hand out to shake.

Jess shook his hand and they both sat down, Jess on the other side of his desk. He handed him the wanted poster on Myer Bollington.

"I'm looking for this man," said Jess, "but the man at the livery said he rode out two days ago?"

"Yeah, he did, but I didn't know he was wanted," declared the marshal. "Seemed like a really nice fella and all."

"I don't suppose you know which way he headed out of town?"

"No, I was out checking on a sheep rancher who has been having trouble with a pack of wolves attacking his stock."

"I understand you own the hotel in town?"

"I do, and if you want a room, it's on the house."

"Thanks," said Jess as he stood up.

"Tell my wife, Gabby, to give you that fancy suite on the third floor," he said. "It's right next to our living quarters."

"Thanks, I'll do that."

He walked out of the jail and looked at the livery, where he saw Carl Savage riding up to the front of it. He sighed and headed for the hotel.

When he walked in, a woman who looked particularly homely smiled at him, revealing two buck teeth that had to be far enough apart to hold a peppermint stick in place.

"I see you must be a lawman or bounty hunter," she said. "I saw you coming out of the jail where my husband is the marshal."

"Bounty hunter. He said to put me in the suite next to your living quarters."

"You'll like that room," she said as she handed him the keys.

He handed her a five-dollar bill and she frowned at him.

"I'm sure he meant for you to stay as our personal guest, so you don't have to pay for the room," she said as she held out the bill to him.

"Oh, that's not for the room, that's for you to maybe buy that dress you've had your eyes on or something else you might want."

She blushed and smiled.

"Well, that's a very nice gesture, sir," she said as she stuck the bill into the pocket on her dress. "Actually, I have had my eye on a blue-and-yellow dress over at the women's clothing store for some time now."

"Well, I'd say go and get it now, while it's still there," he told her.

"I will," she said. "I'll get one of the housekeepers to cover for me while I go and get it."

Reedy

He walked up the steps to the third floor and found the room. When he opened the door, he was surprised to find a huge living area with a large bed, all kinds of furniture, a large bathtub and even a private privy in the corner with a hand pump and bucket.

The bathtub had two pump handles on it, and he wondered what they were for. He put his things on the bed and washed his face with water from the bowl on the bureau.

Deciding to get a meal before taking a bath, he walked out, locked the door and headed down the steps. When he reached the bottom, he saw Carl Savage standing at the counter, checking in to the hotel.

He had his rifle in one hand and his small set of saddlebags hanging across his left shoulder. He smiled at Jess.

"I tried to get a room close to yours, but she said you're on a private floor," said Savage. "I couldn't even get one with a bath in it."

Jess looked at the woman behind the counter.

"Why does the bathtub in my room have two hand pumps close together?" he inquired. "Is it to fill the tub faster?"

"Oh. no," she explained. "We have a two-hundred-gallon metal basin on legs out back and it's always full of hot water with several fires underneath it. The pump on the left is for hot water and the pump on the right is for the cold."

"I'll have to take a look at that," said Jess. "Sounds like something I might want to install in my lake houses."

"You have houses on a lake?" questioned Savage.

"Yeah, three houses on three different lakes."

Savage didn't respond; he simply looked surprised.

Jess smiled at the woman again.

"Best place to eat in town?"

"Millie's Café at the end of Main Street," she said.

"Thanks," he said as he walked out.

Savage paid for the room and got the key. He went to his room and opened it. He put his things on the table and grunted.

"Lake houses?" he muttered. "I really don't know this man at all."

CHAPTER THIRTEEN

Jess ate a meal at Millie's Café and it was delicious. He left a nice tip on the table and walked out. As he headed back to the hotel to take a nice hot bath, he looked at a place called the Fish Inn Tavern.

The place had a painted picture of a large fish on the front of the building. He was about to go inside to see what they served, but before he took one step, a familiar face stepped out through the batwing doors.

Jess sighed and shook his head. He walked to the middle of the street in front of the inn and stopped. The man popped a cheroot between his lips and struck a match on one of the posts holding up the overhang. He took in a long drag and blew the smoke out through his nostrils.

"Well, if it ain't the infamous Jess Williams," he bellowed loudly. "The man they say can't be beat on the draw. I say that theory is about as fake as you are."

"Alton Crawford, biggest windbag and braggart west of the Mississippi," said Jess. "I see you haven't changed one bit."

"And obviously, neither have you."

"I never made those claims about me; other people did."

Jess noticed Savage moving along the boardwalk, toward the tavern, listening and watching with curiosity. He stopped and leaned against one of the posts holding up the overhang.

A few of the locals and two of Crawford's friends came strolling out after hearing the loud exchange. Crawford saw them and felt emboldened.

"I suppose you're here to show off your pistol skills?" scoffed Crawford. "You gonna twirl that fancy pistol you got there? You want I should throw a silver dollar up in the air and see if you can put a hole in it?"

"I only pull this pistol out when I'm going to use it."

"Ahh, I'm shakin' in my boots now," he cackled. "You boys here my bones rattlin'?"

"Crawford, why don't you shut that piehole of yours and move on, before you push this too far," Jess cautioned him.

"Did you hear that?" he bellowed. "He just threatened me. I don't know. Maybe I gotta respond somehow?"

"Yeah, you show him, Crawford," said one of his friends behind him. "He ain't nuthin' special."

"Maybe I should come over there and box your ears a good one," threatened Crawford, as he opened and closed his fists a few times.

"I wouldn't try that," warned Jess.

"Why, you afraid of battling it out with fists?"

"No, I just don't do it."

"Oh, so, if I come over there and punch you in the face, you ain't gonna hit me back?"

"You'll never punch me in the face."

"Sure, I can," he bragged. "I just gotta walk down these steps, walk straight up to you and punch ya."

"I know how it's done, but you simply won't make it," explained Jess. "Now, finish your smoke, go back inside and have another drink with your friends."

"See? What've I been tellin' you boys all along. He's nothing but a coward hiding behind a false reputation that has been built up by stories and rumors."

Jess shook his head slowly and sighed. He looked at the belligerent man again with distain.

"Crawford, I've met rocks that ain't as dumb and ignorant as you are. Now, shut up or prove to your friends how tough you are."

"I'm gonna do just that," he bellowed. "And when I'm finished, I'm gonna show them your teeth that I'm about to knock out of your smart mouth."

Crawford started down the steps and began walking toward Jess, who removed his hammer strap, causing his two friends on the boardwalk to remove theirs. Crawford didn't even notice it. He kept walking toward Jess.

"You'd best stop right there," cautioned Jess as he moved his hands into position by his gun.

Crawford grunted, and took one more step, which was one too many.

Jess slicked out his pistol and fired one shot that shattered Crawford's left kneecap. He wailed and went down on his rear in a dusty thump.

His two friends in front of the saloon went for their pistols, but Jess fanned two more shots. One slug hit the first man in the stomach and the second slug slammed into the other man's sternum.

Both men smashed against the front wall of the saloon and slowly slid down into sitting positions. All the other men raised their hands in the air.

The man who took the first slug to the stomach squirmed around, screaming in pain. The other men moved away from him. Jess fired again. The slug entered his chest dead center and nicked his heart. He quickly stopped moving.

Crawford, on the other hand, was screaming and holding his shattered kneecap. He glared hatefully up at Jess.

"You shot me and I didn't even try to go for my gun," he complained.

"Like I said before, dumber than a rock," said Jess. "How many times did I warn you? I remember three times myself. But did you listen? No, because you're a windbag who doesn't have a lick of sense in his entire body."

"Someone, help me up and get me to the doctor," he yelled painfully.

A few men started stepping off the boardwalk and Jess shook his head at them.

"The only place he's going is to the undertaker's parlor to be fitted for a pine box," Jess told them.

Crawford looked up at him worriedly.

"What do you mean by that?" he asked nervously.

"You think I'm gonna let you live so you can come and find me later and ambush me or try to shoot me when I'm sleeping? I'm not stupid like you and your friends were, who are both dead now by the way, thanks to you."

"But…but…I'm not dead like them," he wailed.

"Not yet you aren't," Jess said as he cocked his pistol and fired once more.

The slug rammed into Crawford's forehead, knocking him backward onto his back. He let out his death rattle as his head rolled to one side and he became stone-still.

Marshal Lemon came running over with a shotgun in his hands. He shook his head as he looked at Crawford.

"That boy's been itching for a fight since he got to town," declared Lemon. "Looks like he found one. Just not the one he wanted."

"So, you've got no problem with what happened here?" Jess asked him.

"Nah, that's three troublemakers I don't have to deal with now," declared Lemon.

Jess replaced the spent shells in his pistol as the undertaker showed up with a wagon and a helper. He tipped his stovepipe hat at Jess.

"Mr. Williams," he said.

Jess nodded to him and headed to the tavern. When he walked up the steps, all the local men moved aside to let him pass. He stopped momentarily to look at the two dead friends of Crawford.

Then, he glanced over at Savage, who was still leaning against the post, his eyes glued on him. He walked inside through the batwings.

Immediately, he smelled the odor of fried foods and the distinct odor of fish. The owner of the place, Woody Gibson, walked out from behind the bar and over to him.

"Welcome to the Fish Inn Tavern," he said. "I'm Woody Gibson. Thanks for getting rid of those three troublemakers. That man, Crawford, chased half of my customers away today. He started three fights with the local men and beat the dickens out of them. I really didn't think you'd shoot him though."

"He's been like that since he was a young boy," explained Jess.

"You hungry?"

"I already ate at Millie's, but the smell coming from the kitchen is odd, but in a good way," said Jess as he looked at the menu board.

"Yes, the smell kind of clings to you," admitted Gibson.

"Fish and chips?" Jess asked.

"Well, I'm from overseas," he explained. "London to be precise. There are many fish and chip places there. When I opened this place five years ago, I decided to bring the dish out here with me. We use a batter on the fish before we fry it and we cut the potatoes into thin strips, fry them, and serve them alongside the fish. Most people love it. Would you like to try some?"

"Just one piece of fish and a few of the fried potato strips," he said.

He walked to the bar and Woody poured him a glass of beer. The order of fish came out a few minutes later and Jess let it cool for a minute. Carl Savage walked in through the batwings and up next to him.

"I have to admit, I've never seen anything quite like that before," said Savage. "You just killed three men and the marshal thanked you for it."

"Like I told ya, things are different here than out East," explained Jess. "Too many outlaws and way too few lawmen to control them. Crawford and his pals would have just continued to cause trouble. Eventually, they would have killed someone, if they haven't already. Truth is, I probably saved someone's life today, although I don't know who. Maybe a woman, maybe a man, or maybe a young boy or girl."

"You have a strange way of looking at things," admitted Savage.

"It's just the way life is out here," Jess said. "A poor dirt farmer could walk into a saloon after working his place for sixteen hours because he just wants a drink before he goes home to the missus. Five minutes later, he's lying dead on the floor in a pool of his own blood for something as little as bumping into an outlaw. If the town has no law, and many of them don't, nothing is usually done about it. But, if that outlaw gets his face on a wanted poster that says dead or alive, well then, I hunt him down, end his life and most likely, save the next person he would have killed."

"And shooting that man who was going to punch you? He never even removed his hammer strap. In your mind, how do you justify that?"

"I don't fight with my hands," said Jess. "And I warned him repeatedly not to attempt to hit me. If I had let him do that, he probably would have beaten me to death or close to it. Who would I be able to save after that?"

"Seems a bit conceited on your part, don't you think?"

"Maybe, but I'm in the business of taking the lives of bad men in order to save the lives of the innocent. If some look at that as a bad thing, then I don't know what to say to them, except to ask them, what if it was your wife, your daughter, or your son that a bad man murdered? Would you want me to be there to make sure he didn't kill anyone else's wife, daughter, or son? Or would you rather have me on the ground, beaten so badly that I'd have to give up my line of work, just so no one could say that I shot a man who hadn't pulled his gun on me?"

"That's quite the dilemma. I don't know how to answer it," admitted Savage.

"Well, to tell you the truth, neither do I," sighed Jess. "Now, let me ask you a question."

"Okay."

"If a man came at you with a knife, and he had no other weapon, would you fight him off with your hands or shoot him dead with your pistol?"

"A knife is a deadly weapon and can kill, so yeah, I'd shoot him," admitted Savage. "Maybe just in the arm or leg to stop him though."

"With certain men, fists are just as deadly a weapon as a knife. Many men have been beaten to death by fists. And, if you just wound him, his pride would be hurt and he'd be ashamed to show his face. Here in the West, that man would wait to find you sleeping or walking along the street and shoot you dead when you're not looking. Now, who's the bad man?"

Savage hung his head in deep thought. He finally looked up and sighed.

"That's quite another dilemma, isn't it?" he said.

"Yeah, it is, ain't it?"

Jess broke the piece of fish in half and took a bite. He chewed and swallowed. He looked over at Savage, who was obviously still deep in thought.

"You gotta try this fish," said Jess. "It's really delicious."

CHAPTER FOURTEEN

Frank Reedy waited in his office until an hour after dark to see if the two deputies from Calico showed up. They didn't. He finally donned his hat and headed for the telegraph's office.

When he arrived, Melvin was sitting on his bench, waiting for his next assignment. He looked up at Reedy and when he saw the look of concern on his face, he didn't tease him. Reedy handed the operator the message he had written down in his office earlier.

"This has to go out to Judge Hood in Calico," Reedy told the operator.

"Sure thing, Marshal," he said.

He sent the message out and handed it back to Reedy, who dug into his pocket to pay Melvin, but Melvin waved him off.

"No, I can see something is wrong and you're worried," said Melvin.

"Thanks, Melvin," said Reedy. "You're a good kid."

Reedy went back to his office and opened one of the drawers on his file cabinet. He grabbed three Deputy United States

Reedy

Marshal badges and dropped them into his front shirt pocket, where his badge was pinned on.

He headed for the Stratton Hotel and walked into the fancy mahogany bar where Henry usually worked. Henry was sitting at a table with some of the prominent people of the town. He looked over at Reedy.

"I've seen that face on you before, Frank, and it's never a good thing," said Henry.

"No, I'm afraid it's not," admitted Reedy as he walked to his table. "I'm here to ask if I can deputize one of your personal guards to assist me."

"Sure, anything you need, Frank," said Henry. "How about Calvin Shuster? He's tough as they come and good with a gun."

"He'll do just fine," said Reedy.

Henry looked at Shuster, who was sitting at a table with one of Henry's other guards.

"Calvin, the marshal needs you," he said.

Shuster was a large-framed man and strong as an ox. He wore a double holster and was good with either hand. He stood up and walked over to them.

"What do you need me to do, Frank?" Shuster asked.

"Raise your right hand and repeat after me."

Shuster didn't question him; he simply raised his right hand. Reedy swore him in and then took out one of the badges from his pocket and pinned it on Shuster's left shirt pocket.

"You are now officially a Deputy United States Marshal. We leave at daylight," said Frank.

"Yes, sir," said Shuster. "I'll be waiting in the livery for you at first light."

"Good," said Reedy.

Shuster walked back to the table and sat back down with the other guard.

Henry saw the worried expression on Reedy's face again.

"Those two deputies from Calico never showed up, did they?"

Reedy shook his head.

"No, they didn't, and I expect the worst," said Reedy.

"Judge Hood is a very important friend. We need to do whatever we can to make him happy," advised Henry. "So, anything you need, men, money, anything, you'll have it."

"Thanks, Henry. I know I can always count on you."

***

Jess woke at the first signs of daylight. He took the time to take a hot bath, got dressed and put on all his weapons. He left the hotel and when he walked into Millie's Café, Savage was finishing his morning meal.

He walked over to the table and sat down next to Savage so he had a clear view of the front door and windows.

Savage looked at him curiously.

"Decided to sleep in?" he asked Jess.

"No, I took another hot bath in my room."

"Oh, I forgot you have that fancy suite on the private floor."

"Yeah. I looked at that basin of hot water behind the hotel and I'm having one built for each of my houses on the lakes."

"You really have houses built on lakes?"

"Yeah, and I built the lakes too, although I hired the right people to create them."

"Are you a rich man?"

"I suppose so."

"Then, why the hell are you out here hunting down killers? Why not retire and go from one house to the next and just relax and enjoy your money?"

Jess sighed and looked at him.

"I don't know," he answered. "I guess it's kind of hard to do that when I know there's some killer out there murdering an innocent person for no real reason. It's just in my blood to do this work. Someday I'll hang up my guns and retire. Maybe even marry. But not yet. Not until I eliminate more killers from this world."

"But why you? Why do you have to do it?"

"Because I'm best suited for it," he explained. "I can track a man across solid rock. I have an extra sense of danger that most men don't. I can kill a man from over eight hundred yards out with one of my Sharps buffalo rifles and I've got two horses that can outrun any other horse out there, unless they came from the same stock. They were specially bread and trained to run long distances and for longer times than most."

"So, you think you were destined to do this work?"

"I don't know. What I do know is after my family was brutally murdered, I started practicing with my pa's pistol. Then, one day, out of thin air, appears this pistol and holster I'm wearing now. I don't know where it came from, but no one has seen anything like it before. When I started using it, I became faster and faster with it. When I was ready, I headed out to hunt down the three killers. Now, here I am today, still doing it."

"That's an interesting story, with no probable answer," said Savage.

"I suppose not," admitted Jess.

The door to the café opened and the telegraph operator walked inside. He glanced around, spotted Jess, and headed straight for him. He held out a slip of paper.

"It's from United States Marshal Frank Reedy and it said it was important."

Jess took it and handed the man a silver dollar. He unfolded it and read the message. His face turned serious and Savage noticed it.

"Bad news?" he asked.

Jess shrugged his shoulders.

"Not yet, but it might end up being bad news. My friend, John Bodine, who is the town marshal of Stratton, has the vicious killer, Ned Malone, locked up in his jail. Two deputies were being sent from Calico to pick Malone up and take him to Calico, where a Texas state supreme court justice is waiting to hang him personally for killing his wife. Seems they didn't show up on time. My other friend, United States Marshal Frank Reedy, is going out looking for the two deputies."

"Okay, so what does that have to do with you?"

"Nothing yet, but I might get called into service again before it's over."

"Why you?" he asked. "You're a bounty hunter."

Jess pulled the Deputy United States Marshal badge from his front pocket and showed it to him. He dropped it back in.

Savage grunted.

"Jeez, I just keep finding out more things about you that I never realized."

"Yeah, well, I'm not far from Stratton here, so I'll stay and wait until I find out what happened."

"Looks like I'll be staying around too," said Savage.

"There's nothing keeping you here, except your decision to challenge me."

"Oh that? I've given up on that idea, now that I know more about you," admitted Savage.

"Then why stick around here?"

"I don't know," he said. "Maybe you'll need my help?"

"What makes you think I'll need your help?"

"I don't know," he said. "Maybe you're not the only one with an extra sense for something."

Jess grunted and waved at the waitress. He ordered and ate his meal. Savage got up and walked out of the café. Jess watched him with curiosity.

The waitress brought him his food and he sat there eating, wondering what Frank Reedy would find out about the two missing deputies today.

He sensed that something bad had happened.

***

Frank Reedy and Calvin Shuster rode out of Stratton at first light. They rode along the well-used trail going to Calico. They stopped several times for the horses to rest. While they were walking the horses, Shuster looked over at Reedy.

"Maybe those two got sidetracked somehow," reasoned Shuster. "There's a trading post about five miles east of this trail that has two whores working there."

Reedy shook his head.

"Those deputies were under the direct order of a state supreme court justice," he explained. "They wouldn't get sidetracked by anything."

"Maybe so," said Shuster.

Then started the horses at an easy gallop again, Reedy watching the left side of the trail, Shuster watching the right. They had ridden about five miles when Reedy halted his horse.

Shuster reined his in and turned in the saddle.

"See something?" he asked.

Reedy pointed up at the sky.

"That can't be a good sign," said Reedy.

Shuster looked up at the sky and saw huge vultures circling.

"Nope, that's never a good sign," he admitted.

Reedy

They started the horses again and when they got closer, they spotted the two horses wandering around in the fields, munching on whatever they could find. They slowed the horses to a walk and saw the bunch of vultures in two piles, fighting each other for their piece of the meal.

Reedy slid out his rifle and fired two shots into the air. The large birds began flapping their huge wings and soaring up in the air, screeching as they did.

They rode over to the bodies, which were already quite ripped apart. Reedy leaned on his saddle horn.

"Well, can't see their faces anymore, but their badges say deputy marshal of Calico, Texas. They were obviously ambushed."

"How can you be sure?"

Reedy looked over at him.

"What do you think the odds are of two healthy men dying of natural causes at the same exact time?"

Shuster nodded.

"I see your point," he admitted.

"Malone is known to have a gang working with him," said Reedy as he looked around the area.

He saw the copse of trees off to one side of the trail and pointed to it.

"Let's go and have a little look-see in them trees," he told Shuster.

They rode over, dismounted and began walking around.

"What are we lookin' for?" Shuster asked.

"Expended rifle cartridges," said Reedy.

Shuster caught a glint of something and bent down. He picked up an expended rifle cartridge and held it out to Reedy.

"You mean like this?"

Reedy walked over and took it from him.

"Yep, that confirms it," he said.

"They walked around some more and found another expended cartridge and then found two sets of horseshoe prints in the soft soil.

"Two horses, two shooters," declared Reedy.

"Any guesses as to who they were?"

Reedy shook his head.

"I remember some of the names of Malone's gang of thugs, but there's no way of knowing which ones of them did this," advised Reedy.

They walked back out to the bodies. Reedy pulled the badges off the two torn and tattered shirts. He stuck them into his pocket with the other two federal badges and then they collected the horses.

"Are we gonna bury them out here?" Shuster asked.

"No time," said Reedy. "They already murdered the two deputies on their way to get Malone. We need to get back to town and protect the jail in case they're planning a jail break. I don't know how many men Malone still has working with him."

They climbed up in the saddle and headed back to Stratton.

CHAPTER FIFTEEN

Reedy and Shuster arrived back in Stratton toward the latter part of the afternoon. They rode straight for the jail. After dismounting, they walked inside the jail to find Bodine sitting behind his desk, a sawed-off on his desk within reach. He looked up at Reedy and sighed.

"It's bad news, ain't it?" Bodine asked.

"Both of them were dead, ambushed by two men out on the trail on the way here," said Reedy as he plopped down in one of the chairs.

"I see you brought their horses back, but not the bodies," said Bodine.

"Vultures literally tore them apart," said Reedy. "Wasn't much to bring back. Had to just leave 'em there. No time to bury 'em either."

Shuster stood by the heavy door going to the back cells. He looked through the small barred window to the cells and saw Malone lying on a cot, sleeping.

"What's the plan now?" Bodine asked.

"Well, we have to get Malone to Calico, one way or another," said Reedy.

"Why not just hang him here?" inquired Shuster. "Or put him in front of a firing squad."

"Because State Supreme Court Justice John Hood wants to hang him personally in Calico," said Reedy.

"And a supreme court justice gets what he wants," added Bodine.

Reedy turned in the chair to Shuster.

"Go get some sleep," Reedy told him. "I'll need you ready first thing in the morning."

"And what if Malone's men try to break him out of the jail?" queried Shuster.

"We'll defend the jail as best we can. Reinforcements will arrive within seconds to help."

"All right," said Shuster as he walked out and headed for the Stratton Hotel.

Bodine looked at Reedy.

"I kind of like his idea of the firing squad," said Bodine.

"There's nothing more I'd like better than to go in there and empty my gun in that rotten bastard," said Reedy. "But we have to get him to Calico. Get the keys to the cell door."

"You want to talk to Malone?" Bodine asked.

"Yeah."

"He's not gonna tell you squat, Frank. He's already sentenced to death. He has nothing to lose at this point."

"Well, talking is free, so let's go talk to him."

Bodine got the keys off the peg on the wall and stood up. He unlocked the heavy door going to the back and Reedy followed him inside. Malone didn't get up; he simply opened his eyes and grunted.

"Something go wrong, fellas?" he asked contemptuously as he slowly sat up on the cot.

Malone was skinny with a pockmarked face and dark beady eyes that were too close together at the top of his crooked nose.

"Two of your men murdered two deputies from Calico who were coming to transport you there to be hung by Judge John Hood."

"How do you know it was two of my men?"

"Who else would have had a motive to kill 'em?"

"Hell, I'm not the only outlaw in Texas," he said. "You boys ain't got enough lawmen to catch 'em all. It could have been anybody who done it."

"How many men do you have out there, Malone?" asked Reedy.

"Hell, I'm not sure," he answered. "It could be two, three, four, maybe more. My boys sign up other men at times. Why don't you just let me go and save yourselves a lot of unnecessary trouble and grief?"

"You're not gettin' out of this one, Malone," said Reedy. "You're gonna swing from the end of a rope while the judge watches you gasp for air."

"You'll never get me to Calico, Reedy. You're one of the toughest, meanest lawmen I know, but even you can't get me there."

"I'll get you there, even if I have to take you there myself," declared Reedy.

"Oh really?" asked Malone. "The big man is gonna escort me himself?"

"If that's what it takes, yeah, I'll deliver you there myself, along with some help."

"Good luck tryin'," scoffed Malone.

He lay back down on his cot and closed his eyes.

Reedy turned to Bodine.

"He gets nothing but bread and water from here on in," Reedy ordered.

Malone sat up quickly.

"You can't starve me," he groused. "I got rights as a prisoner."

"You lost those rights when your men murdered those two deputies from Calico," exclaimed Reedy.

"You can't prove it was my men what done it."

"I don't care if I can prove it or not," spat Reedy. "You're all out of lucky breaks."

Reedy and Bodine walked out of the cell area and Bodine locked the heavy door. Bodine looked at Reedy, who seemed angrier than he had seen him in quite some time.

"Frank, I'm not so sure you should be the one taking him to Calico," he said.

"I won't be going alone. I'll have Shuster and one more of Henry's personal guards joining me on the trip."

"How 'bout we send for some Texas Rangers instead?"

"That'll take weeks for them to get here, if they can spare two, that is. And the longer we wait, more of Malone's men could join up with the others. We're leavin' Stratton first thing in the morning and gettin' this done, once and for all."

"All right, but I don't like this one bit, you goin' on this escort. You know that Malone's men hate you with a passion. You've locked most of 'em up at one time or another, including Malone."

"I can't let fear stop me from doing my sworn duty," said Reedy. "Besides, I don't believe his men will think we'll move him tomorrow morning. They'll figure on a few days from now."

"All right," agreed Bodine. "I'll have him ready tomorrow morning. I'll have your horse and his brought to the front of the jail at first light."

"I'll send out a wire to the judge letting him know we're on our way tomorrow and let him know about the two deputies who were murdered."

"Should I send the undertaker out to pick up the remains and put them into pine boxes?"

Reedy sighed and shook his head.

"Might as well wait for the vultures to finish their job," he answered. "Anyone riding that trail between here and Calico could end up dead. Maybe the undertaker from Calico can determine which man is which, depending on the size of bones that will be left. I'll let him know when we get Malone to Calico."

"All right then, Frank," said Bodine.

Reedy headed for the telegraph office and sent a long message out to Judge Hood in Calico, with a note of attention to Jess, informing him of the two dead deputies and what was happening next. When he finished, he went to the Stratton Hotel to talk to Henry about another guard to ride along tomorrow.

***

Vic Walter and Tad rode back into their hidden encampment after gunning down the two deputies from Calico. When they arrived inside the wooded area, they found Willie French sitting at the fire, sipping some whiskey. Everyone had taken to calling him Frenchy. He wore a left-hand gun and long black hair.

"Where have you two been?" Frenchy asked. "I've been waitin' fer two hours now."

The two dismounted and tethered their horses to the line.

"We was out takin' care of business," explained Walker. "That judge in Calico sent two deputies to Stratton to pick up the boss. We killed 'em both, so that should delay them a day or so."

"Does Frank Reedy still keep his office in Stratton?" Frenchy asked.

"Yeah, he does," replied Walker.

"Well, if I know Reedy, he ain't gonna wait no day or two," proclaimed Frenchy. "I'll bet this last bottle of tongue oil that he'll move the boss first thing in the morning."

"Ya think so?" asked Tad.

"Reedy ain't just tough as rawhide; he's smart too, and he'll think like us," advised Frenchy. "We'd best get out ahead of him and whoever else he's bringin' along."

"We've got a few hours of daylight left, so let's head out now and make camp," suggested Tad. "We can find another spot to ambush them from. They'll be watching those trees we used today."

They broke camp and rode out along the trail to Calico. When they reached the small copse of trees they had used before, they saw that the vultures had pretty much cleaned the last of the meat from the bones of the two deputies. They made a cold camp and fell off to sleep.

CHAPTER SIXTEEN

Jess spent the day in Galantine, wandering around the town, checking things out. When he came across a gunsmith's shop, he stopped in and showed the man the custom-loaded fifty-caliber cartridges for his buffalo rifles.

"Where did you come up with this idea?" he inquired.

"From a man who was trying to kill me with one of 'em."

"I can make some of these for you," he said.

"Can you get fifty of them made up before morning?"

"For you, sure," he said. "I'll put my other jobs aside and get to work on these right away."

"I'll pay you double your fee for doing that."

"Thanks," he said.

He walked out and looked at his pocket watch. His stomach grumbled and he headed for the Fish Inn Tavern. When he walked in, Carl Savage was sitting at a corner table, eating. He waved Jess over. He walked across the room and sat down at the table.

You're right about this fish," said Savage. "It's delicious."

Reedy

"Yeah, I'm gonna get an order myself."

The telegraph operator walked in and looked around. Once he saw Jess, he headed straight for their table.

"This had your name on it along with Texas State Supreme Court Judge John Hood," he said as he handed it to him.

"More bad news?" Savage asked.

Jess finished reading the message. His face took on a more serious expression as he did. He handed the operator a silver dollar and sighed.

"My friend, Frank Reedy, found the two deputies' bodies from Calico out on the trail. He's informed Judge Hood that he's escorting Ned Malone with two of Henry Stratton's guards to Calico for the hanging."

"Ain't that good news?" asked Savage.

"Maybe, maybe not. Frank is as tough and smart as they come, but no one knows exactly how many men are still loyal to Malone. I'd bet anything that it was some of Malone's gang of thugs who murdered those deputies who were on their way to Stratton to pick him up."

"So, doesn't that solve the problem?"

"I'm not sure, but I'm heading to Stratton first thing in the morning."

"You want me to come along?"

"Why would you want to do that?"

"I find you a very interesting man with a very interesting life."

"Well, I can't tell you where to go, but I leave at first light and I'm not waiting for you," Jess told him. "Frank is a very close friend of mine and I won't be delayed one minute getting there."

Jess ordered the fish and they sat there, eating in silence. Savage was wondering about Jess's friendship with this Frank Reedy fellow.

Jess was hoping he could catch up to Frank before anything bad happened. After they finished eating, Savage went to the bar and Jess went to the hotel to get ready for the ride to Stratton in the morning.

***

Frank Reedy had gotten Henry Stratton to let him deputize another of his personal guards, Ewing Tinker. Tinker was as tough as Shuster and asked no questions, except for when to be ready in the morning.

Reedy had supper delivered to the jail for Bodine and himself. They would lock themselves in the jail for the evening and Henry would have two of his men take turns at watch on the front porch of the hotel during the night in case a jail break was attempted.

Bodine had already put the heavy manacles on his desk and had the livery owner in town set to deliver Reedy and Malone's horses to the jail at first light. He and Reedy were sitting in the jail, discussing the trip in the morning.

"I figure it's a two-day ride to Calico, hauling a prisoner," surmised Reedy. "We'll make cold camps with no fire and eat beans and jerky until we arrive in Calico."

"Sounds like a good plan, even though I don't like you leading the escort," cautioned Bodine.

"It's my job, John. You know that as well as I do," said Reedy. "You escorted Malone from Fulton to the jail here all by your lonesome."

"That may be true, but now his gang knows exactly where he is and where he's going. Is there a different route you could take?"

"Yeah, but that route is rough terrain. It would take us three or four days to get to Calico going that way," Reedy explained. "And it has more ambush spots for them to attack us from."

"Well, let's hope it goes well," said Bodine. "Let's get some shut-eye now and wake at daylight."

The two got in the cots in the front office and fell off to a light sleep.

As soon as light filtered through the front windows of the jail, Reedy woke and reached over to nudge Bodine.

"Time to get up," said Reedy as he sat up and yawned.

Bodine slowly got up and walked to the front window on the door of the jail. He turned to Reedy, who was standing up and stretching his back.

"Horses are already saddled and ready in front of the jail," announced Bodine. "I'll make coffee and we can eat some leftover biscuits before you leave."

"That's fine with me."

They were finishing the coffee and biscuits when they heard a light rap on the door. Bodine got up and walked to the front door to see Shuster and Tinker standing there, rifles already in their hands. He opened the door.

"You boys want some coffee before you head out?" Bodine asked.

Shuster shook his head.

"We're fine," he said. "We'll be waiting right out here with our horses."

"Okay," said Bodine as he left the door open on purpose.

Reedy put his hat on and picked up the manacles from the desk. Bodine opened the heavy door going to the cells to find Malone sitting on his cot.

"Did you do your business yet?" Reedy asked.

"I took a leak, but I don't need to shit, since you boys ain't fed me in two days now," he grumbled.

"You can survive weeks without eating, as long as you get water," said Reedy. "Now, back up against the wall."

Malone stood, backed up and placed his back against the wall. Reedy gave him a serious warning look.

"You're gonna put your hands together in front, and if you try anything at all, you won't like what happens next," warned Reedy.

Bodine unlocked the cell and then levered a round into his rifle. He opened the cell door, walked to Malone and put the barrel of his rifle against his privates. Malone eyeballed the barrel of the rifle and then looked at Bodine.

"Yeah, I really will do it," Bodine told him flatly.

Reedy

Malone put his hands together with his fingers thrust out. Reedy walked to him. He put the manacles on his wrists as tightly as he could.

"Now, sit down on your cot," ordered Reedy.

"What for?"

"Just do it," said Reedy.

Malone sat down and Bodine stood to one side and aimed the rifle at Malone's privates again. Reedy pulled his boots off, one at a time.

"How am I supposed to ride a horse without boots?" questioned Malone.

"Oh, I'm sure you'll have blisters by the time we get there, but it won't matter much anyway," said Reedy. "Now, stand up and let's go outside."

Malone walked out of the cell area and out the front door, where he was met by two men who already had their rifles aimed at him.

"I must be important to get all this attention," said Malone.

"Yeah, but you won't be so important after they walk you to the gallows in Calico," said Reedy. "Now, get on your horse."

Malone put his foot in the stirrup and grabbed the saddle horn with his two hands. Once he was in the saddle, Reedy tied his ankles to the stirrups. He turned to Shuster.

"Shuster, you take the lead by fifty yards and keep your eyes peeled for ambush points," explained Reedy. "I'll follow behind you with Malone's horse tied to the back of my saddle."

He turned to Tinker.

"You follow me by twenty-five feet. If you hear one gunshot ring out, you shoot Malone in the back of the head."

Malone snapped his head over to Reedy.

"But what if it's just someone huntin' rabbits nearby?" asked Malone.

"Well then, I guess you'd better pray that no one along the way is hungry for rabbit," grinned Reedy.

Shuster climbed up in the saddle and started along the street. Reedy tied the reins to Malone's horse to the back of his saddle and climbed up on his horse. He rode behind Shuster.

Tinker swung up in the saddle and kept his rifle at the ready. Two more of Henry's men stood on the front veranda of the hotel with rifles in their hands.

Bodine stood on the boardwalk in front of the jail and watched them until they were out of sight. He sighed and slumped his shoulders slightly.

"I got a bad feeling about this," he whispered to himself as he headed for the telegraph office.

He sent out a wire to Judge Hood in Calico, telling him that Reedy was escorting Malone to Calico and should arrive in two days.

CHAPTER SEVENTEEN

Jess rode out of the livery in Galantine just as the light of day was making its first appearance. He had rousted the gunsmith out of bed to get his custom-loaded fifty-caliber cartridges for his buffalo rifles. His plan was to eat in the saddle while his horses walked to rest.

Carl Savage was just coming out of the hotel when he saw Jess ride out of the livery. He shook his head and headed to Millie's Café for a quick bite before heading to Stratton himself.

Jess kept his horses at an easy pace for the first half hour, but once the sun was up enough to provide plenty of light on the trail, he urged them along at a fast pace.

He didn't normally switch up on the horses, but needing every second and every mile, he started rotating, riding Gray and then Sharps and back again.

While he was resting them by walking, he opened a can of beans and ate them cold from the can. He hadn't come across any creek or streams by the noon hour, so he stopped and used his hat to water his horses from two of his canteens.

When he finished that, he waved his hat around to dispense the leftover water in it and donned it before climbing up on Sharps and walking the horses for a bit longer to let them rest again. He hoped to keep this pace up all day, which would get him to Stratton right around dusk.

Back in Galantine, Carl Savage rode out about a half hour later, following the tracks left by Jess's two horses. After a bit, he could tell that Jess's horses were running fast and for longer distances than his before taking breaks.

"His horses sure can run long," admitted Carl.

***

Calvin Shuster led the escort by about fifty yards. His rifle already had a shell chambered and the hammer released. He held it in his right hand and rested the barrel on the pommel of the saddle.

He stopped often to look through his field glasses, watching for any trouble up ahead, expecting the worse, hoping for the best.

Frank Reedy rode behind him, the reins to Ned Malone's horse tied to the back of his saddle. Malone's shackled hands were tied to the saddle horn on his horse.

Ewing Tinker brought up the rear, his rifle in his hands. He was always turning in the saddle to check their back trail for any signs of trouble.

He was a man who followed orders, so at the first signs of an ambush, he would shoot Malone in the back of the head without hesitation or remorse.

Reedy

When Shuster first saw the copse of trees off the trail, he halted his horse and put his left hand up. He peered through his field glasses and Reedy rode up next to him. They looked at the bones of the two deputies off the trail.

"Vultures and critters done picked their bones clean," said Reedy.

Shuster lowered the field glasses and looked over at Reedy.

"How 'bout I go and take a look-see in those trees?"

Reedy nodded.

"Go ahead. We'll cover you as best we can," he said as he held his rifle in his hands.

Shuster rode slowly toward the trees. When he reached them, he slid from the saddle and walked into them. After finding the camp the outlaws had used the night before, he looked around at the horseshoe prints and boot prints.

He saw several empty cans of beans and peaches on the ground, along with one empty whiskey bottle. Picking up the bottle, he tipped it over and saw the drops coming out of it.

"They stayed here last night," said Shuster.

Throwing the bottle on the ground, he strolled out of the trees and walked his horse toward Reedy.

"The good news is they stayed here last night and moved on farther along the trail," he explained.

"And the bad?" queried Reedy.

"Looking at the tracks I found in those trees, there are three of them now, so one of Malone's other men must have caught up to the other two."

"The fact that they're smart enough not to use this spot for a second ambush means they're planning on attempting another one up ahead on the trail, so we have to be extra vigilant," Reedy explained.

Shuster climbed back up in the saddle and moved ahead to take the lead again. Reedy let him get about fifty yards ahead before starting his horse. Tinker stayed close enough behind Reedy to be able to kill Malone at the first signs of an ambush.

***

Walker, Tad, and Frenchy had ridden out of the copse of trees they had used to ambush and kill the two deputies from Calico at first light. They rode along the trail, searching for a good spot for an surprise attack. They finally found it in a heavy grouping of mature scrub oak off the trail by about thirty feet.

They rode to the scrub oak and dismounted. After looking around, Walker shook his head.

"This will work for us, but there ain't enough cover here for the horses," said Walker as he turned to Frenchy. "Take the horses out behind us far enough so they don't see them."

Frenchy looked out at the landscape and saw some tall bushes way off in the distance. He grabbed the reins to the three horses and started walking them out to them. When Frenchy returned, Walker looked at him.

"If I know Reedy, he'll have a man in the lead to scout the area and a man taking up the rear, so we need our best shot to take out the man in the rear," explained Walker. "Frenchy, that's your job. Me and Tad will take out whoever else is in the escort. We don't know how many men we're dealing with, but we all take our first shot at the same exact time."

Frenchy looked at Walker.

"You say when," said Frenchy. "I'm gonna move to the far end of this cover so I'm closer to the man in the rear."

"All right then," said Walker as he and Tad took up positions to fire from.

The three of them waited patiently, hoping they had made the right decision, thinking Reedy would have their boss moved immediately. Walker was standing up and taking a leak when Tad first saw the lead man appearing around a bend in the trail.

"Hey, I see a man coming along," whispered Tad.

Walker buttoned his pants and got down on his knees again. He peered through his field glasses and watched as the second man appeared at the bend. Walker focused his field glasses better and grunted.

"That second man is Frank Reedy himself, hauling our boss behind his horse," said Walker excitedly. "Oh, and there's a man in the rear. Frenchy, put your sights on that man. Tad, you shoot the lead man and I'll kill that sumbitch Reedy myself. Wait for my signal."

Shuster was walking his horse slowly now because of the bend in the trail. As soon as he made it around it, he spotted the scrub oak up ahead. He halted his horse and put his left hand up to stop the others. Reedy stopped and then so did Tinker.

Shuster peered through his field glasses and kept looking around at the scrub oak. It wasn't that tall and he didn't see any horses anywhere. He lowered the glasses and turned in the saddle.

"I don't think anyone is hiding in there since I don't see any horses," he explained. "But let's approach it slowly as a precaution."

Shuster started his horse again, followed by Reedy, Malone, and then Tinker. Reedy suddenly felt a knot in his stomach. He didn't know why, but he called out to Shuster.

"Shuster, hold up for a minute," he called out.

In the scrub oak, all three men had their targets in their sights and their fingers on the trigger. Walker's lips curled up into a devilish smile as he put more pressure on the trigger of his rifle, which was aimed directly at the federal badge on Reedy's shirt pocket.

"To hell you go, you sonofabitch," he whispered to himself. "Now!"

Three rifle shots rang out simultaneously. The slug from Tad's rifle slammed into the center of Shuster's chest, knocking him sideways off his horse. He landed hard on the ground.

The slug from Walker's rifle punched straight through Reedy's United States Marshal badge. The force of the impact knocked him off the back of his horse.

Tinker was raising his rifle to shoot Malone in the back of his head, but the slug from Frenchy's rifle went through Tinker's right cheekbone, bounced upward and traveled through his brain. He slumped over and slowly fell off to one side of his horse.

Reedy

Shuster attempted to get up and grab his rifle, but three slugs put him back down for all eternity, never to move again.

Reedy and Tinker were on the ground, motionless. Walker, Tad, and Frenchy walked out of the scrub oak with their rifles held high.

Malone smiled evilly as he looked down at the blood forming on Reedy's shirt around his badge.

"Cut me loose and let's get the hell outta here," he shouted.

Frenchy ran to him, pulled out his bowie knife and cut the ropes from his ankles and wrists. Malone dismounted and walked to Reedy's body. He fished around for the keys to the manacles and found them.

Walker walked to him and used the keys to unlock the manacles and Malone rubbed his wrists. He looked at the boots on Reedy's feet and grunted.

"Get his boots for me," ordered Malone. "They look like my size."

Walker pulled them off Reedy's feet and Malone pulled them on. He looked at the hole in Reedy's badge and the blood forming around it. He smiled and grunted.

"The law didn't save you this time, you bastard," carped Malone. "Let's get the hell out of here."

"Our horses are almost a mile back that way behind those bushes," said Frenchy.

"Grab these three horses and ride them to yours," ordered Malone as he untied the reins to Reedy's horse and climbed up in the saddle.

The other three men swung up on the horses and the four of them rode away at a gallop toward where they had left their horses. When they reached theirs, they left the other horses there and the four of them rode off across the terrain, following no trail.

CHAPTER EIGHTEEN

Jess was tired and trail-weary when he finally reached the busy town of Stratton. Some of the townsfolk waved or nodded to him. He headed straight for the livery at the end of Main Street. When he got his horses inside, he slid from the saddle.

The owner saw who it was and smiled.

"Mr. Williams, glad to see ya finally back here."

"Yeah, it's been a while," said Jess.

The man looked at the dried sweat on the two horses.

"You've been riding 'em hard, eh?"

"Wash 'em down, brush 'em and feed 'em well," said Jess. "Is Frank Reedy in town now?"

"No, he left here this morning with two of Henry Stratton's guards, escorting that prisoner to Calico."

Jess exhaled heavily. He looked at his pocket watch and grunted.

"Have my horses saddled and ready to ride at midnight," Jess told him.

"Midnight?"

"Yep. Just enough time for me to get a hot meal and some shut-eye before I hit the trail to Calico."

"Well, okay, if you say so," said the owner.

Jess handed the man more than enough money, then headed out of the livery and straight for John Bodine's office. When he got there, the door was unlocked and no one was inside. He peeked through the small barred window of the heavy door going to the cells in back. They were empty.

When he walked out of the office, Bodine was standing on the veranda of the Stratton Hotel, waving at him to come over.

He walked across to the hotel and frowned at Bodine.

"Why did you let Frank go on that prisoner escort?" Jess asked pointedly.

"Well, nice to see you too," huffed Bodine. "And why in a million years do you think I could talk Frank out of doing something he done made up his mind to do?"

"I suppose you're right," admitted Jess. "But Malone is dangerous and crafty, and his men all hate Frank with a passion. We know there was already one ambush that cost the lives of the two deputies from Calico."

Bodine slumped his shoulders and sighed.

"Listen, there wasn't any way I could've talked Frank out of going. I tried, you know I did, but he's as stubborn as he is tough. He took two of Henry's best guards with him though."

"I'm leaving just after midnight to ride along the trail to Calico."

Reedy

"You're gonna ride at night?"

"The moon will be out then and I can walk my horses until daylight. I can cover maybe four to five miles an hour. I need to catch up to them as soon as I can, hopefully before another possible ambush."

"Well, come on in and get a good hot meal," said Bodine.

Jess followed him in to the fancy mahogany bar that Henry was standing behind.

He smiled nervously at Jess.

"I'm not surprised you're here," admitted Henry as he walked out from around the bar.

He walked over to the table where Bodine had a half-eaten plate of food. Bodine and Jess sat down as he reached them.

"I'll have them bring you a plate of food right away," said Henry. "Now, what are you planning?"

"I'm gonna fill my belly, get some sleep and leave at midnight, following the trail Reedy and your men took with Malone."

"I still have two good guns left at the other hotel on the lake," said Henry. "Both of them are yours if you want them."

Jess shook his head.

"No, they'll never keep up with me when daylight comes," said Jess.

"I thought you'd say that," admitted Henry.

He snapped his fingers and a waiter appeared almost instantly.

"Get Mr. Williams whatever he wants to eat and arrange for one of the best rooms on the first floor for him to sleep in," Henry ordered. "Wake him at midnight."

"Yes, sir," said the waiter as he smiled at Jess. "What would you like to eat, sir?"

Jess looked at the meatloaf on Bodine's plate and nodded to it.

"I'll take the same thing he's eating."

"Coming right up, sir," said the waiter.

Bodine smiled at Jess.

"Good choice," he said. "Joy makes this meatloaf twice a week and it's always delicious."

His plate of food showed up at his table in a few minutes. He took a bite and chewed. He ordered coffee to drink. He looked up at Bodine.

"I can't be certain, but a man by the name of Carl Savage might show up in town later," said Jess.

"Never heard that name before," said Bodine. "Is he gunnin' for you?"

"He was, but now he just wants to…I don't know really," admitted Jess. "Study me?"

"Huh?" asked Bodine, a confused look on his face.

"Let me guess," said Bodine. "He's from out East?"

"Yeah, he heard about me and traveled out West to find me and challenge me, but he changed his mind after he learned a few things."

"You want me to lock him up and hold him here?"

Jess thought about it as he chewed the meatloaf.

"Nah, I don't think he's any threat to me. I think he wants to help, although I don't know why."

"Want me to tell him where you went?"

"I think he's figured that out already."

"Jess, you look tired," said Bodine. "You sure you don't want to sleep all night and leave in the morning?"

He shook his head.

"No, I got a bad feeling about this whole thing," said Jess.

"Yeah, me too," confessed Bodine. "It's been gnawing at my gut all day long."

Jess finished his meal, took a few gulps of coffee and stood up.

"I'd better get some shut-eye before midnight comes."

"I think I know the answer, but do you want me to go with you later?"

"No, you stay here," Jess told him.

Jess went to the room Henry had arranged and Bodine went back to the jail. He was about to lock up the office an hour or so later, when he saw a lone rider heading straight for the jail. He locked the door and turned to wait for the man.

"You must be Carl Savage?" he asked.

"Yeah, how'd you know?"

"I'm John Bodine, town marshal. Jess told me you might be following him."

"I tried, but at least I didn't have to breathe in any dust from his trail," said Savage.

"Yeah, his horses move fast," chuckled Bodine. "They stop fast too. I've gotten thrown out of the saddle on Sharps more than once."

"Where is Jess now?"

"He's over at the hotel. He's sleeping a few hours and leaving town at midnight. Moon will be out then."

"He's gonna track at night?"

"Not unusual for him, but he knows the trail they took, so he'll just follow it until daylight. Then he'll put them long horses into a dead run like the devil was chasin' 'em."

"Well, I'm hungry and tired," sighed Savage.

"The restaurant is still open at the hotel and you can get a room there too. You planning on following Jess tonight when he leaves?"

"No, I'm bone-weary from trying to keep up with him today," he admitted.

"He told me you were thinkin' about challenging him?"

"Yeah, but I gave up on that idea."

"Good thinkin' on your part 'cause he'd put you in an early grave for sure," said Bodine.

"I saw him work that pistol of his back in Galantine," said Savage. "I don't think there's a man on either side of the Mississippi who could come close to beating him."

"Everyone who's tried so far has ended up dead," said Bodine.

"Well, I'm gonna stable my horses, eat a hot meal and get a room for the night."

Reedy

"All right then," said Bodine.

He took his horse to the livery, stabled it and headed to the hotel. He ate, got a room and fell off to sleep at soon as his head hit the pillow, exhausted from the long ride.

Savage was fast asleep when Jess opened his door and walked out. He headed out of the hotel and to the livery, where his two horses were already saddled and ready to ride. The owner of the livery was already sleeping in his house behind the place.

He walked his horses out of the livery and climbed up in the saddle. He rode along Main Street. It was eerily quiet, even in the saloons.

He found the trail leading from Stratton to the town of Calico and started walking his horses along the trail. The moon was already coming up and shedding silvery moonlight over the land.

He rode quietly along the trail as the moon crossed the sky. As he glanced up, he wondered how many more people would be looking up at it at the same time.

He closed his eyes a few times, snoozing for a minute here and there. As he snoozed, his ears listened for any sounds that didn't fit the normal ones for this time of the night.

As daylight made its first appearance for the morning, he ate a piece of cornbread he had saved from supper and drank from one of his canteens until it got light enough to run his horses.

He put the canteen back on his saddle horn, patted Gray on his neck and sighed. He looked over at Sharps, who bobbed his head up and down as if to say, I'm ready.

"Sorry, boys, but we gotta move fast again," said Jess as he tapped his heels against Gray's flanks.

The two horses dug in their haunches and took off like an arrow let loose from a bow. Within seconds, their strides were lengthened and they were moving like the wind.

A few hours later, he was walking his horses to rest them when he spotted vultures circling in the air way up ahead on the trail.

He slid his rifle out of the scabbard, levered a round into it and released the hammer. Urging his horses into a dead run again, he leaned forward in the saddle and kept his eyes peeled.

A few of the vultures began to come down closer and he suddenly heard a rifle shot ring out, which made him halt his horses.

Taking his spyglass out, he extended it and peered through it, but saw no bodies up ahead on the trail. He saw where the trail took a bend to the left.

"Who the hell took that shot and why?" he said to himself as he continued to peer through the spyglass.

CHAPTER NINETEEN

Jess, unsure of who took the shot and where it came from, dismounted. He took his spyglass and rifle and moved to where the bend in the trail began to make the long turn. The first things he saw were the two bodies on the ground, far apart from one another.

Extending the spyglass, he saw the glint off the badges on the shirts of both dead men. He saw the scrub oak, moved the spyglass over to it and peered through it.

The lenses were powerful enough that he could see fine details in the scrub oak. After searching them for a minute or so, he finally saw some movement.

The first thing he saw was a rifle barrel leaning against a branch. Then, he saw a slight movement of what looked like an upper torso. He closed the spyglass, stuck it into his back pocket and raised his rifle at the body.

"Who the hell is in there?" he shouted.

Hearing no immediate response, he shouted it out again.

"I see someone in that scrub oak, a rifle and two dead bodies," he yelled. "Identify yourself or I'll start throwing lead!"

"Jess, is that you?" asked a voice that sounded familiar.

"Frank?"

"Yeah, come on over here and bring some water and your medical kit."

"Show your face first," said Jess.

Pulling the spyglass out of his pocket again, he extended it. Reedy stuck his face out through the branches and Jess saw it was him. He could tell from the long curly blond hair and salt-and-pepper mustache and trimmed beard. He closed the spyglass and ran back to his horses.

After sliding the rifle into the scabbard, he put the spyglass away and jumped in the saddle. He heeled his horses into a run toward the scrub oak and jumped down from the saddle.

Grabbing a canteen and his medical kit, he walked into the scrub oak to find Reedy sitting Indian style and looking a little weary. Jess knelt beside him. He saw the hole in his shirt pocket and the dried blood.

"How bad are you hit?"

"Not as bad as I could've been," answered Reedy as he pulled out the badges from his front shirt pocket.

He handed them to Jess. The slug had penetrated the first two badges he had in his pocket and was sticking out through the last badge about a quarter of an inch.

"Jeez, Frank," he said. "You are one lucky badge toter."

He dropped the badges back into his front pocket.

Reedy

"Yeah, the slug punched through the skin enough to bleed so they thought I had bought it. The other two weren't so lucky. I've been scaring off wolves, coyotes and vultures from the bodies since the ambush. Ain't had but a few hours of sleep."

Jess handed him the canteen. He took sips from it as Jess opened his medical kit. Reedy unbuttoned his shirt and lowered it. The badge had left a jagged gouge on Reedy's chest that would leave a permanent scar. Jess chuckled.

"There's nothing funny about it," chided Reedy.

"Maybe not, but it'll serve as a reminder of the foolish decision to transport Malone when you knew some of his men had already ambushed the deputies from Calico."

"Oh, yeah, here comes the lecture," he grumbled.

"Well, you should have told me to come and help instead of trying this foolhardy move."

"And what would you have done differently?"

Jess stopped for a few seconds to think about it.

"Most likely, I'd go out and search for ambush spots on this trail to Calico. Then I'd use my buffalo rifles to kill his men from a distance before they ever laid eyes on me."

"Yeah, well, maybe I should've waited for you to arrive," he admitted, begrudgingly.

"Well, at least you're alive," said Jess. "I'll clean this up a little and bandage it. There's a trading post called Barny's nearby. We can go there and get it properly cleaned and stitched. And, we can check to see if Malone and his men are there or maybe stopped there."

"It's been a full day since they ambushed us, so they're probably quite a distance from where we are now. By the way, how'd you get here so fast?"

When I heard you were going to escort Malone, I hightailed it out of Galantine and got to Stratton at dusk. I ate, slept till midnight and walked my horses in the moonlight all night. Come morning, I put my horses into a hard run until I reached here."

He finished working on his wound. Reedy pulled his shirt up and buttoned it. He stood up and grabbed his rifle. They walked out to the bodies and Reedy collected the badges, putting them in the other front shirt pocket.

Jess looked at Shuster's socks.

"Did someone take his boots?" he asked Reedy, pointing to Shuster's feet.

"No, Malone took mine and I took Shuster's. They're a little big on me, but they'll do for now."

Jess looked around some more.

"They took your horses?" Jess asked.

"No, they're way out behind us by some bushes," Reedy said as he pointed.

Jess looked out at the three horses, wandering around the fields. He turned back to Frank.

"I'll go round them up and bring them back here. We can load their bodies and leave them with the man at the trading post. We can wire Henry when we hit the first town and he can send a wagon to pick them up and give 'em a proper burial in Stratton's cemetery."

Reedy

"Agreed," said Reedy as he looked at the two dead men, shaking his head again.

Jess packed his medical kit and climbed up in the saddle. He rode out to the bushes and took a few minutes to study the tracks leaving the area.

After retrieving the horses, he brought them back to where Reedy stood. He and Jess loaded up the two dead bodies on their horses and tied them down tightly. They climbed up in the saddle and headed for the trading post.

It didn't take long for them to get close enough to the post for Jess to scan it with his spyglass. The trading post didn't have a barn, only a large lean-to for horses to stay out of the weather. He put the spyglass away and looked at Reedy.

"It looks like there's no one at the post at the moment," said Jess. "But let's not take any chances. We've been following Malone and his men's tracks all the way here."

They both slid their rifles out and walked the horses the rest of the way. Jess kept scanning the area around the post, but it was mostly barren land with bushes here and there. After riding to the front of the post, they slid from the saddle.

"These are the tracks of Malone and his three men in front, so let's be slow and careful," advised Jess.

Reedy put his back to one side of the door and Jess did the same on the other side. Reedy reached over and slowly turned the handle on the closed door. It moved.

"It's not locked," he whispered.

Jess readied himself and nodded to Reedy, who shoved the door open and rushed in, moving to his left immediately to allow Jess in next. He moved to the right.

They heard muffled sounds coming from behind the long makeshift bar. Jess kicked the door shut with his boot heel and the two of them walked toward the bar, rifles held high.

Jess kept glancing at the two doors to his right where there were private sleeping quarters for guests. When they reached the bar, Reedy walked around it to see a fat, grubby-looking man tied to a chair that was tipped over.

His mouth was bound and gagged. Reedy put his rifle on the bar, went behind the man and lifted the chair upright.

He took a folding knife out of his pocket and cut the rope holding the gag in and the ropes holding his hands and ankles.

The man spat the gag out and took in a few long breaths. He saw the badge on Reedy's shirt and smiled.

"Thank goodness the law finally showed up," he said. "Four men came here yesterday, took all my cash and some of my supplies and left."

Reedy gave the man a complete description of Ned Malone and he nodded his head rapidly.

"Yeah, he was the one giving the orders."

Jess carefully checked the guest rooms. They were empty. He lowered his rifle and walked to the bar, where the man was now standing, leaning on both hands. The man was short, fat and had long straggly hair.

"How much cash did they take?" Jess asked him.

Reedy

"Everything I had, enough to make it through the winter months," he moaned. "Eighty dollars and some loose change."

Jess pulled some bills from his pocket, picked out a hundred-dollar bill and set it on the bar in front of the man.

His eyes widened.

"What the hell is this for?" he asked Jess.

"To make up for what they took, and to pay you for your services and the things we'll need to take."

"My name is Barny. So what do you need me to do?"

"We have two dead United States Marshals on their horses outside," Reedy explained. "We need you to hold their bodies here until some men from Stratton can come and pick them up."

The man snatched the bill and smiled.

"I can do that," he said. "You boys hungry? I have rabbit stew on the stove in the back."

"Yeah, we can surely eat," said Reedy.

"You two want to stay the night?" he asked. "You only have a few hours of daylight left. I have hay in the lean-to outside for the horses and rooms available."

Jess looked questioningly at Reedy, who nodded.

"We're both tired. I need a few stitches and we can supply up and head out in the morning," said Reedy.

"I agree," said Jess. "You let him stitch you up and I'll take care of packing the saddlebags and taking care of the horses outside. You got a place for us to store the bodies?"

The man nodded and pointed to the back.

"There's a door on the back of the building where there's a small shed that'll keep 'em till they get here," said the man.

"We'll have to leave three horses behind too," Jess told him.

Reedy looked confused.

"Why are we leaving my horse behind?"

"Because you'll be riding Sharps instead," Jess explained. "Henry's men will take your horse back to Stratton when they come for the bodies."

"All right," agreed Reedy as he started taking his shirt off, while the man got his medical bag out to stitch up the wound.

Reedy never flinched when Barny sewed the wound shut after pouring some alcohol in it to sanitize it properly.

Jess gathered supplies, packed the saddlebags and took care of the horses. He untied the two bodies from the horses and put them into the shed off the back of the building.

Then he went inside and ate with Reedy. They turned in after that so they could get an early start in the morning.

CHAPTER TWENTY

Ned Malone and his three men had ridden hard after they left Barny's trading post. They had packed up plenty of supplies and walked their horses during the night to gain as much distance as possible, knowing the law would be coming after them.

The next day, they rode just as hard, heading in a straight line as much as possible, sometimes leaving the trail and crossing empty land and riding over hills. Taking every precaution, they had passed two small towns without going near them.

When they crested one hill, they saw the forest below and Malone gave the signal to halt the horses. They looked around the area and saw nothing but a small stream running through a large meadowland of heavy grass and entering the forest.

"I think we just found a place where we can rest up for a day or so," said Malone.

Vic Walker looked over at him.

"We just murdered three United States Marshals and one of 'em was Frank Reedy," cautioned Walker. "Reedy is highly regarded in the Marshals division and has connections in Washington. I wouldn't be surprise if they sent the U.S. Cavalry after us."

"Well, let's get down there and set up a camp deep inside those woods," said Malone. "I'm hoping we can catch or trap some fish in that stream."

"I got me one of them small nets to string across the stream to catch 'em," said Frenchy.

"Good," said Malone. "We can save on food supplies then."

They rode down the hill and through the meadow, then entered the forest. It was slow going, having to break branches off to make a path through the dense forest. They followed the stream and eventually the trees thinned out some, with fewer small trees in the way.

Once they found a clearing, they dismounted and looked around. It was close to the stream and large enough for them to set up camp.

Walker, Tad, and Frenchy started taking care of everything. Frenchy dug a hole for the fire and collected plenty of dried branches. Walker tended to the horses and Tad took the net and strung it across the stream.

Malone took off his boots and used more of the salve he had taken from Barny's Trading Post to rub on his blistered feet and ankles that were blistered from riding his horse without boots.

"Damn that Frank Reedy to hell," he cursed.

Frenchy, who was fanning the flames with his hat, looked over at him.

Reedy

"Well, you done made him pay," he grinned. "Shot that bastard right though his badge and, hopefully, hit his cold heart."

"Yeah, may he burn in hell forever," said Malone.

Tad brought back a lot of fish that he had already cleaned at the edge of the stream. They fried and ate them, along with some fried potatoes. They turned in early, not having had any sleep the night before. Because they were so deep into the forest, they kept the fire going all night.

***

Back at Barny's trading post, Jess was just getting dressed when he heard horses approaching outside. Barny was in the kitchen in back, frying bacon. He didn't hear the horses.

Three rough-looking men dismounted and looked around. They couldn't see the horses in the lean-to from their angle, so they assumed no one was inside except for the owner. The lead man in the outfit was called Boss by the other two men.

Two of the men were about the same size and height, except for the man they called Boss. He was muscular and large-framed, reaching close to six feet in height.

One of the two men had a heavy mustache that covered most of his mouth. The other one talked with a high-pitched squeaky voice, garnering him the nickname, Squeaky. He turned to Boss.

"Well, Boss, what do you want to do?" he asked in his high-pitched, squeaky voice.

Boss looked around and saw the smoke coming out of the metal stack on the roof.

"I smell bacon cookin'," he declared. "Time to eat and decide what else to do after that. Don't look like anyone else is around, so I suppose we can do whatever we want."

The man with the mustache looked at the hand-painted sign over the front door.

"The place is called Barny's, so I reckon the man inside is Barny," he said.

Boss looked over at him, shaking his head slightly.

"Ain't you the smart one?" he said.

Mustache hung his head and sighed.

Inside his room, Jess slid his pistol into his holster, but left the hammer strap off. He put his ear to the wall to Reedy's room and heard rustling.

Outside, Boss walked to the front door, opened it and stepped inside, his hand on the butt of his pistol. He saw the room was empty. Mustache and Squeaky walked in behind him.

"Anyone in here?" shouted Boss.

Barny lifted his head and put the fork down on the platter. Being quite overweight, he waddled out of the kitchen to see the three rough-looking men. He stopped in his tracks and his smile vanished.

"Uh, you boys hungry? 'Cause I just started cooking some breakfast."

"You cookin' food for someone else?" asked Boss.

Reedy

Barny, fearing another robbery in the very near future, shook his head.

"Uh, no...I'm all alone at the moment," he said in a little louder voice.

Reedy was putting his gun belt on and heard Barny talking.

"Must be more trouble out there," whispered Reedy.

Jess heard it too and he gently cracked his door open just enough to see.

"Well, we all want to eat, so git your ass back in the kitchen and keep cooking," said Boss.

The three of them sat down at one of the tables inside and waited. Barny went back to the kitchen and threw more bacon on the stovetop. Jess peered out through the crack in the door and saw the three men, noticing none of them had untethered their pistols yet.

He reached over and tapped the wall to Reedy's room twice. He heard two taps coming back from the other side, meaning Reedy was aware of the situation brewing in the main room.

Boss heard it and looked over in the direction of the doors going to the rooms. He slipped his hammer strap off and looked at the open doorway to the kitchen.

"Hey, fat man?" he called out.

Barny appeared at the open doorway.

"Yeah?"

"I thought you said there wasn't anyone else here?"

"Uh, there ain't," he said as he waddled farther into the room.

"I just heard some knockin' on the walls somewhere."

"Oh, that's just the rats," he lied. "They climb up and down the walls all the time. They're brave too. I've seen 'em jump up on tables and start stealing bacon right off people's plates. I'd get some cats, but the rats are as big as a cat."

"I don't like rats," said Mustache.

"Shut up," said Boss.

Barny started waddling back toward the kitchen. Boss noticed the wooden crates by the shelves with all the supplies neatly stocked. Then, he looked over at Squeaky.

"Go and get one of those crates and fill it up with supplies," he told him.

Barny stopped waddling and listened.

"But, we ain't got but two bits between us," said Squeaky.

"Who said we was payin' for 'em?" asked Boss.

Barny's shoulders dropped, he sighed and headed back into the kitchen, fearing the worst, and hoping the lawman in the guest room would come out soon.

Squeaky stood, walked over to the wooden crates and picked one up. He began taking canned foods off the shelves first.

After filling the first one, he grabbed another and started putting in things like salt, pepper, flour, cornmeal, a sack of beef jerky and other items. By the time he filled the second crate, Barny waddled out of the kitchen carrying large platters of food.

He looked over at the two crates and then delivered a platter of bacon and flapjacks to the table as Squeaky sat down.

Reedy

"I'll be out with scrambled eggs and all the fixings next and then I'll ring up your purchases," he said nervously.

Boss sneered at Barny.

"That won't be necessary, fat man," he said. "We ain't payin' for nuthin'."

Jess stood just inside the door, shaking his head, and tightening his lips at the audacity of some outlaws.

Reedy was waiting for Jess to signal him or to make a move, but he got impatient and threw his door open. His gun was untethered. He looked at the three men.

"What's this I heard about not payin' for nuthin'?" demanded Reedy.

CHAPTER TWENTY-ONE

Reedy stood there, his right hand on the butt of his pistol, giving the three men a stern look.

Boss, Mustache and Squeaky sat there, looking over at Reedy. The saw the badge on his shirt with the hole in it.

"Who the hell are you?" asked Boss as he slowly stood up.

Reedy quickly noticed the loose and dangling hammer strap over Boss' pistol. His eyes jerked over to the other door as Jess swung it open and stepped out, his right hand hovering over the butt of his unique pistol.

Mustache and Squeaky stood up and shoved their hammer straps off as they did. Jess smiled at Boss, who glared back at him.

"Who the hell are you?" demanded Boss.

Barny, hearing the loud talking, waddled out from the kitchen and stopped in the open doorway.

"I think you need to answer the marshal's question," suggested Jess.

"We got no respect for lawmen," spat Boss. "And we don't recognize their authority none either."

"Well, you might want to rethink that idea," advised Jess.

"And why would we do that?" asked Boss.

Jess nodded over at Reedy.

"Because he ain't just another lawman with a badge," Jess explained. "He is one of the top United States Marshals in the states. He has authority wherever his feet land and that authority doesn't come into question, like a town marshal or a constable."

"I don't know what all them words mean," admitted Boss.

"Let me explain it to you in simple terms that you might understand," said Jess. "See, if he wants to shoot you dead right now, he'll write up a simple report that says he felt the need to shoot you. Now, that report will eventually find its way to Washington, where some clerk will file it in some dusty file cabinet and no one will question it, because he's a high-ranking federal lawman."

Boss moved his eyes back to Reedy.

"So, why does he wear a badge with a hole in it on a bloody shirt?" he asked.

"Oh, he got shot the other day and now he's ready to get back to work again," Jess said as if it was nothing more than a mosquito bite.

"So, you think that makes him tough?"

"Think? Oh no. I know he's tough. I would suggest you three get on your horses, ride on out of here and don't look back. Otherwise, Frank there is gonna shoot you, and I'm gonna shoot your pals there."

Boss scoffed and grinned.

"You think we're afeard of you two?"

"It doesn't matter," said Jess. "You go for those guns and you die. Is that simple enough for you?"

Boss took that comment as an insult and it showed on his angry face. He grunted and went for his gun.

Jess's hands moved in a blur. He shot Mustache straight through the heart and Squeaky in the right side of his chest, blowing out one lung.

A second later, Boss had his gun mostly out of his holster and the hammer half-cocked when the slug from Reedy's pistol punched a hole through his throat. He let the pistol drop back into his holster and grabbed his throat with both hands.

Mustache hit the floor loudly. His arms and legs spread out like a boy making a snow angel in the wintertime. His gun never left his holster.

Squeaky, on the other hand, had jerked his gun out as a reflex action when the slug slammed into him. His gun flew across the floor and stopped when it hit the leg of a chair. He was moaning and squirming around in pain, gasping for air.

Jess looked over at Reedy, who was already replacing the spent shell in his gun. Jess walked to where Squeaky lay, groaning in his high-pitched voice. He cocked the hammer on his unique pistol again and aimed it at the man's chest. Squeaky put his hand out and shook it back and forth.

Reedy

"No, no, you can't shoot a wounded unarmed man like this," he moaned as he looked over at Reedy, who was holstering his pistol.

"He'll have to write one of them reports and you ain't wearing no badge like him, so it'd be murder, not self-defense," claimed Squeaky.

Reedy grunted and started walking toward the bar.

"Not if I don't see it," said Reedy.

Squeaky looked back at Jess as he slowly pulled his federal badge out of his front pocket and showed it to him. He dropped it back into his pocket.

"This ain't happening because I have this badge," Jess told him.

"Aw, hell," wailed Squeaky.

Jess pulled the trigger. The slug broke through his sternum, punctured his heart and found a new home in the wooden floor underneath Squeaky. His body arched for a second and then fell flat against the floor. His death rattle slowly escaped his lips as his head fell to one side.

Jess replaced the spent shells in his pistol, holstered it and turned to see Reedy at the bar, sipping coffee. Barny stood there, motionless, staring at the three dead bodies.

Reedy turned at the bar.

"Let's haul 'em out of here before they stink up the place," he said.

Jess and Reedy hauled the bodies out and dropped them way behind the trading post. When they finished, they went inside, washed up and sat at the table where Barny had set the platters of foot, along with a coffee pot.

"What do you want me to do with the three new dead bodies you just hauled out?" asked Barny.

"Well, by the time Henry's men get here, the vultures will have made quite a mess out of 'em, so I'd just let them and the other critters finish 'em off," advised Reedy. "We don't have time to dig three graves. We have four dangerous outlaws to catch."

"Uh, okay then," said Barny. "I'm too fat and clumsy on my feet to do it myself."

"Don't worry yourself over it," Jess told him.

They finished eating and Jess turned to Reedy.

"How's your chest wound?"

Reedy turned to him and grunted.

"I'll worry about that once Malone has that rope around his slimy neck," he said.

"Same old Frank Reedy," Jess chuckled.

The two stood up, shook hands with Barny and headed out of the trading post. Jess brought the horses around to the front of the post and Reedy rubbed Sharps' forehead.

Jess swung up on Gray and Reedy climbed up in the saddle on Sharps, who bobbed his head up and down.

"Remember, he takes off fast and stops even faster," cautioned Jess.

"I remember. Now, let's start tracking those killers."

Reedy

Jess rode around the front of the trading post and found where the four sets of tracks left by Malone and his men headed away. He looked over at Reedy.

"We'll ride slow at first to see if they make any turns. If they stay straight, we run 'em hard and fast."

"Obviously I'm goin' wherever you're goin'," said Reedy.

Jess kept the horses at an easy canter and after a few miles, the tracks stayed straight in one direction. He looked over at Reedy, who was staring straight ahead.

"They're cutting a straight line to cover as much distance as they can in a day," Jess told him. "Let's pick up the pace now. Hold onto your hat."

Reedy nodded and pulled his hat on tighter, leaning forward in the saddle. Jess urged his horses into a dead run. In just a few seconds, they were galloping at a breakneck speed.

"Damn," said Reedy as he leaned forward a little more, listening to the fast and rhythmic beating of hooves on the ground.

CHAPTER TWENTY-TWO

It was getting later in the afternoon when Jess noticed that the tracks they had been following had come across a well-used trail that continued in a straight line for several miles.

When the trail veered off to the left, he put his hand up to warn Reedy that he was stopping the horses.

"What is it?" Reedy asked.

"The tracks left the trail we've been on and continued straight," he answered as he got out his map of the area.

He looked at it and saw the town of Blunden several miles farther along the trail. He looked at Reedy.

"If we follow the trail we've been on for a while, the town of Blunden is only several miles away. We can send that message to Henry Stratton about his two men we left at the trading post."

"Okay, we can go there, send the message and come back here to follow the tracks a little farther before we make camp," suggested Reedy.

Reedy

"Or we could stay in town and get your wound cleaned and rebandaged by a doctor."

Reedy touched the badge on his shirt and grunted.

"Okay, that's probably a good idea, but we come right back here in the morning," agreed Reedy.

Jess nodded, put the map away, and the two of them continued along the trail leading to Blunden.

***

Abe Baxter stood in the saloon called Ludington's Lair on Main Street in Blunden, Texas. The owner of the place, an older skinny man who had moved from Ludington, Michigan, renamed the place after buying it.

Baxter was a skinny man, considered by many to be good-looking, with a square jaw, clean-shaven face and bright blue eyes.

He leaned on the bar with his elbow, smoking a fat cigar, blowing the smoke up in the air. He had been in town for several days now, hoping for some excitement to happen, but nothing did, so he was planning on leaving in the morning.

A shiny, nickel-plated Colt Peacemaker rested in a black cross-draw holster, forward of his right hip. The butt of the gun faced to his left side. He drew the Colt with his left hand and he was considered one of the best.

He had roamed the coastal towns of Oregon for most of his adult life. His cocky attitude had drawn the ire of many a gunslinger who eventually challenged him, only to find out he was much faster, easily sending them to their grave.

He had hoped that traveling to Texas he would find better challenges, but so far, none had presented themselves, and he was getting bored. He turned toward the owner and barkeep, Huey Mullen.

"Pour me another whiskey," sighed Baxter.

Mullen got the bottle of fine whiskey and poured a little into his glass. He frowned at Baxter.

"I see you couldn't get any players for the high-stakes poker game you wanted," said Mullen.

"No, this town is boring, with nothing exciting happening," grumbled Baxter as he set the cigar on the edge of the bar.

"It's always been a quiet town," explained Mullen. "That's why we don't need a town marshal. If we have trouble, we call on the county sheriff. His office is only a short ride away from here."

***

Jess and Reedy reached the outskirts of Blunden. They sat in the saddle at the end of the main street, observing the people moving about.

"I've been here before. It's always been a nice quiet town," acknowledged Reedy.

"Well, I don't see a hotel, so we either stay in the saloon on the main street or find a boardinghouse," said Jess.

"Hopefully, they still have a doctor in town," said Reedy.

Jess started the horses again and headed for the livery at the end of the street. They dismounted in front and Jess walked the horses inside to find a young man working.

Reedy

He turned around and saw the badge on Reedy's shirt.

"What happened to your badge, mister?" he asked.

"I got shot," said Reedy.

The man walked closer.

"Oh, a federal marshal," he declared. "Never met one before."

"Any boardinghouses in town?" Jess asked.

"Uh, no, but we have two saloons in town that rent rooms. The one on main street is the best one. Huey Mullen owns the place."

He turned his attention to Jess.

"You shore gotta lot of guns, mister," he observed.

"Bounty hunter by trade," he explained.

"A Deputy United States Marshal and a bounty hunter riding together?" he asked.

"Yep," said Jess. "Take good care of the horses."

He handed the young man money, which he gladly accepted.

"Do you still have a doctor in town?" Reedy asked.

"Over on Second Street, at the far end."

Thanks," said Reedy as he looked at Jess.

"I'll go to the doctor's office and you get us some rooms over at the saloon," he told Jess.

"I'll send that wire off to Henry first about his men at the trading post," said Jess.

"Telegraph office is at the other end of Main Street," said the livery worker.

They walked out. Reedy headed for Second Street. Jess headed toward the other end of Main Street. He saw the pole and wires behind a building and veered toward it.

Inside Ludington's Lair, the barkeep and owner, Huey Mullen, was standing behind the bar with his arms folded at his chest. When he saw Jess walking along the street, he unfolded his arms and leaned forward.

"Well, if that ain't Jess Williams, the bounty hunter himself, walking along the street," he said in a soft voice.

Baxter, who was taking a sip of his whiskey, turned at the bar and saw the shotgun handle sticking up over Jess's shoulder.

"Who is Jess Williams?"

Mullen looked at him.

"You've never heard of Jess Williams?"

"No, should I have?"

"Well, he's the best bounty hunter and man killer west of the Mississippi."

"Really?"

"Every man who has ever tested his right hand has found the quickest path to hell."

"Well, maybe this town ain't so boring after all," said Baxter before taking a sip of his whiskey and setting the glass down on the bar.

Mullen looked at him, caution plastered all over his face.

"Oh…uh…you ain't thinkin' about confrontin' him, are you?"

"Why not? I haven't had a good challenge since I left Oregon and came to Texas."

"You'd best pass on this one and wait for someone else to challenge 'cause Williams will put you in the grave before you figure out what went wrong."

"No one can be that good," scoffed Baxter.

"Is everyone in Oregon lunkheaded?"

Baxter frowned at him.

"Why don't you tend to serving drinks and leave the professional gunslinging to me?"

Mullen raised his eyebrows and tightened his lips.

"Yes, sir, Mr. Baxter," he sighed. "I'm shuttin' my piehole."

Jess sent out a long message to Henry Stratton, explaining everything in detail, especially where his two men were. He added Judge Hood to the message.

He paid the operator and walked out. He saw the Ludington Lair and headed for it, slipping his hammer strap off before he reached the steps.

When he walked in, he found two local men sitting at a table and one man standing at the bar, eyeballing him.

He strolled to the bar and the owner walked over to him.

"Welcome to my place, Mr. Williams," said Mullen. "Whatcha in town for?"

"I'm hunting down some dangerous men who passed by your town the other day."

"No one new has come through here in the last few days," said Mullen.

"I'll need two rooms for the night."

"Two rooms?"

"Yeah, the man I'm traveling with is over at your doctor's office."

Mullen handed him two keys and Jess paid him more than enough. He noticed the man to his right, paying him more attention than normal. Jess put the keys in his front pocket and turned to Baxter.

"Have we met before?" Jess asked him.

"No, never," replied Baxter.

"You don't happen to know a man by the name of Ned Malone, do you?" Jess asked as his right hand floated toward the butt of his unique pistol.

"Never heard that name before," admitted Baxter. "Never heard your name before either, until the barkeep here told me who you were."

Jess saw the fancy holster and the gun resting in it. Then he glanced at the barkeep, who shrugged his shoulders slightly.

"What else did you tell him about me?" Jess inquired.

"Only that you were the man to beat in Texas," blurted Baxter before the barkeep could respond.

Jess shook his head slowly.

"Well, that's not good," he said.

CHAPTER TWENTY-THREE

Ned Malone sat by the fire with his boots off. They were slightly tight on him and bothered his blistered feet some. Tad was watching him.

"Those boots bothering you?" he asked.

"A little," admitted Malone. "I should have gotten a new pair at the trading post. I guess I just liked the idea that I left Reedy dead with no boots on."

"Yeah, I git yer meanin'," said Tad.

"Why don't you go relieve Frenchy from cuttin' that escape path outta here?" said Malone.

Tad stood, went to his saddlebags and got out his hatchet. He walked to the edge of the clearing and entered the open pathway. It turned to the right after several feet and then turned to the left again and then began heading in a straight line.

Malone had told them to do it that way so it wasn't easily found. It would give them an extra minute or so to get a head start out of the clearing if they were discovered.

Walker busied himself making more coffee.

When it was finished, he carried the pot to Malone and filled his cup for him. Malone took a sip and sighed. Walker sat back down on the dead tree trunk he had moved into the clearing.

"That's a lot of work we've been puttin' into clearing that path out of here," said Walker.

"Yeah, well, it'll give us a few minutes head start and that might mean the difference between getting caught or getting away."

"I suppose so," admitted Walker. "I'll go relieve Tad in a bit."

"First, go out to the other side and take a gander out at that meadow and hill we rode down to get in here," said Malone as Frenchy came into the clearing.

"I can see out to the other side now," declared Frenchy.

"What's out there?" Malone asked.

"More of that meadowland," he said. "As far as the eye can see."

"How much longer are we gonna stay here?" Frenchy asked.

Malone shrugged his shoulders.

"I'm thinkin' we should leave here tomorrow or the next day," said Malone. "My feet are feeling better."

Walker picked up the field glasses and headed out to the opening they had made to enter the trees. He stood there, scanning the hilltop and the meadowland around it. He set the field glasses down, took out a little bag from his shirt pocket and rolled a smoke.

When he finished, he stuck it between his lips and struck a match on a nearby branch. He lit the smoke, blew out the match and threw it on the ground. Taking in a long pull, he removed it from his lips and blew the smoke out between his lips.

Suddenly, he saw a man walking in front of a donkey. He had a large straw hat on his head. He walked along the edge of the stream and finally stopped.

Walker picked up the field glasses and peered through them. He saw the man dig into his oversized saddlebags and bring out a pan made for panning gold or silver.

The man got down on his knees and began digging the pan into the sediment at the bottom of the creek and swirling the water around in the pan.

Walker finished his smoke, dropped it on the ground and snuffed it out with his boot. He watched the man for another minute or so and then walked back into the woods.

When he reached the clearing, Malone looked up at him.

"See anything we should be worried about?" Malone asked.

"Nah, just some prospector out there with a donkey panning for gold or silver in that stream," explained Walker.

"We'll have to check on him later to make sure he doesn't come in this far," said Malone.

"I'm gonna go relieve Tad out at the pathway," said Walker.

"Frenchy, go check the net for fish," said Malone.

Walker headed out to the escape path. Frenchy went to the stream to get the fish from the net for lunch. Tad came back in and Frenchy brought the already cleaned fish to the fire to cook. By the time he had the grub ready, Walker came back into the clearing.

"I could smell that fish as soon as I got closer," chuckled Walker.

Frenchy handed him a plate and they all ate lunch in silence.

***

Jess stood at the bar, staring back at Abe Baxter, who stood there, eyeballing Jess, wondering just how good he really was.

"How 'bout you show me how fast you are?" asked Baxter.

"Show you?"

"Yeah, you know, draw that gun and let me see your hand speed."

"Now, why would I do such a foolish thing?"

"We've done it in Oregon during our competitions where no one really gets killed."

Jess looked over at the barkeep, who rolled his eyes and shook his head.

"Barkeep, do you keep a map in here?"

Mullen nodded, reached into a cabinet behind him and took out a map of Texas. He opened it and laid it flat on the bar.

Jess smiled at the barkeep.

"Point out to him where we are on the map," Jess told him.

Mullen put his finger on the dot where the town of Blunden was. Baxter looked confused.

"Does that look like we're anywhere near Oregon?" Jess asked him.

Baxter shook his head.

"Well, of course not," scoffed Baxter. "We're in Texas."

"Exactly my point. In Texas, we don't play gunslinging. We do it for real."

"You afraid I'm faster?"

"I'm afraid of no man," said Jess. "I know that one day, someone will beat me and it'll be my turn to take my reserved seat in hell. When it happens, it happens. Worrying about it does me no good."

"I got a hunch that I can beat you," said Baxter.

"There is only one way to find out, but why do it?"

"It is the ultimate challenge, isn't it?"

"It's a senseless thing to do," Jess told him. "It doesn't matter who's faster, does it?"

"To me it does," admitted Baxter.

"Well, not to me. If you go for the gun, you'll end up on the saloon floor in a pool of your own blood, and it'll be your own fault."

Baxter picked up his whiskey and took another sip of it before setting it back down on the bar. He used his right hand to pull the hammer strap from his Colt in his cross-draw holster.

His left hand slowly moved to his gun that rode forward of his right hip. Resting his palm on the butt of it, he drummed three of his fingers on the leather covering the cylinder. Jess moved his hands into position.

Baxter kept staring into Jess's eyes, hoping for a sign or a tell-tale reading, but all he saw was an emotionless, calm expression in them.

"You really aren't afraid, are you?" Baxter asked him.

"Not in the least," he replied.

The drumming of Baxter's fingers on his left hand slowed down, little by little, until they completely stopped. Then, his fingers moved closer to the butt of his Colt and slowly wrapped around it, forming a claw-like position.

His eyes narrowed and his right hand moved behind his side slightly. Then, suddenly, his left arm jerked his Colt out as he cocked it, but his trigger finger jerk-fired the Colt just as the barrel cleared the top of the holster.

The slug from Jess's pistol had already traveled through Baxter's left lung and exited out under his left shoulder blade at his back.

The slug from Baxter's Colt ended up in the front wall of the bar, under the top of it. Baxter's eyes went wide with surprise. The Colt slipped from his weakened grasp as he coughed up lung blood.

His mouth opened and his jaw moved as if he was struggling to say something. Just before his legs gave way, all he said was…

"Damn."

He crumpled to the floor and lay on his left side as he let out his last breath of air from his one good lung. Jess sighed heavily and replaced the spent shell in his pistol as he stared at the body.

Reedy

"Stupid," he whispered to himself.

"Huh?" asked the barkeep.

"Another senseless death, just to prove a point," said Jess.

"Well, you did try to talk him out of it," said the barkeep.

Jess holstered his pistol and looked at the men in the saloon. They were staring at the dead body and the ever-increasing pool of crimson red blood forming on the saloon floor.

The barkeep looked at the men.

"Well, haul his body out of here before he bleeds all the way out," he said.

CHAPTER TWENTY-FOUR

Frank Reedy was buttoning his shirt when he heard the single shot.

The doctor looked surprised.

"Who would be shooting in this town?" he asked.

Reedy gave him a sarcastic look.

"I'm bettin' it was Jess Williams," Reedy told him.

"He's in town?"

"Yep."

"Well, you know, there's been a gunslinger from Oregon way that's been staying here lately."

Reedy handed the doctor a silver dollar.

"I'm bettin' he ain't goin' back to Oregon," said Reedy as he donned his hat and headed out of the office.

He walked to the main street and turned toward the saloon. Two men were putting a body on the ground in front of it. A few townsfolk stood around, staring at the dead body. He slipped his hammer strap off. He reached the two men, who were watching him approaching.

Reedy

"We didn't have nothing to do with this," said one of them when he saw the badge on Reedy's shirt.

"I believe ya," said Reedy as he took the steps up to the batwings.

He walked in and saw Jess standing at the bar, sipping a little whiskey.

Reedy walked up next to him and sighed.

"This is one of the quietest towns I know of and you've been here less than an hour and killed someone already?" Reedy asked.

"He forced that gunfight, not me. I tried to talk him out of it, but he went for his gun."

"He's tellin' it right, Marshal Reedy," interjected Mullen.

Reedy looked curiously at him.

"I know that," he said as he turned back to Jess.

"Well, the doc cut the stitches, checked and cleaned the wound and closed it up again," explained Reedy. "Says I'm gonna be just fine."

"I rented rooms here, so we can turn in early and leave at first light," said Jess.

"Good, 'cause I want Malone back in my custody and delivered to Judge Hood as soon as possible."

"We'll get him, Frank," said Jess.

They stood there and talked about working together in the past, and about all the things going on in Stratton. The development on the lake Jess had created had attracted more and more wealthy and influential people to the town.

They ate supper as soon as it was served. When they finished eating, both went up to their rooms so they could leave early in the morning.

***

State Supreme Court Judge John Hood sat in the café in Calico, Texas, watching the men erect the gallows for the purpose of hanging Ned Malone. He had given special instructions to the carpenters as to how to build it.

He looked down at the message that had been sent out to Henry Stratton and himself regarding the progress on the hunt for Ned Malone.

It explained that Frank Reedy had been left for dead, but was found very much alive and slightly wounded.

It also explained that Jess Williams was now working under Frank Reedy's authority to help track down Malone and deliver him to Calico.

He had never met Jess personally before, but he knew of his reputation for always getting his man. He looked up from the message when the lead carpenter walked in and up to his table.

"Judge, may I sit?" he asked.

"Of course," said Hood as he nodded to the chair opposite him.

He sat down. The waiter brought him a cup of coffee and refilled the judge's cup.

"We're just puttin' the finishing touches on the gallows," explained the man. "It should be done tomorrow."

He saw the message on the table and grunted.

"Any news about Malone yet?"

"He's still on the loose, but Frank Reedy is on the hunt and he has Jess Williams helping him now."

"Jess Williams? The bounty hunter?"

"Yes."

"If Williams is involved, you might not get to hang Malone."

The judge shook his head.

"Frank Reedy has given me his word that he'll deliver Malone alive. I have the utmost trust in Reedy's word and from what I understand, Jess Williams' word is just as good."

"I hope you're right," said the man. "Everyone in this town wants to watch Malone hang for what he did to Cassie. She was loved by all."

"None more than me," Hood sighed.

The lead carpenter took another sip of his coffee and stood up.

"Well, I gotta get back to work out there."

He started to turn around, but Hood stopped him.

"I want you to paint the gallows," he said.

The man turned back to Hood.

"We never paint gallows, because we take 'em apart after they're used."

"I don't care," said Hood. "I want them painted a blood red color. I want Malone to know he's going straight to hell after he's dead."

"Yes, sir," he said. "I'll have it painted blood red starting tomorrow."

"Thanks," said Hood.

He looked out the window again and watched the crew building the gallows. It was the first time one had ever been erected in Calico. His eyes watered up as he thought about his wife and her brutal murder.

***

Jess and Reedy left Blunden at the crack of dawn. They rode to the spot where they had stopped following the sets of tracks left by Malone and his three cronies. The prints were still visible. Jess began tracking them, with Reedy riding beside him on Sharps.

When the noon hour hit, they ate in the saddle as the horses walked to refill their lungs. Jess was eating a biscuit he had taken from the saloon earlier.

Reedy was eating a can of beans. He looked over at Jess.

"Aren't you ready for a rest soon?"

"We're resting now."

"No, I mean a real rest, at your lake house in Stratton," clarified Reedy. "You have housekeepers keeping it clean and Henry has men keeping the place up regularly. Painting it and fixing anything that needs fixing. He had them build a dock in front of your house where two boats are tied. You should go use it for a while."

Jess took a swallow from a canteen and put the cork back in it.

"I've been thinkin' about it, but just haven't found the time for it."

Reedy

"You don't find time for things like that, Jess," he said. "You make time for it. What good is all that money you have if you don't use some of it on yourself?"

"You know that you're always welcome to use the place anytime you want, free of charge. The women will cook and clean up after you. Bodine is welcome to use it too or the both of you together if you want."

"Well, if you ever come to use it, me and Bodine will join you," said Reedy.

"Is that kid Melvin still supplying my firewood?"

"Yeah, he's made sort of a business out of it now," chuckled Reedy. "He supplies Henry all the firewood for the hotel and fish camp on the lake. He's quite the little businessman these days."

"Tell Henry to keep the boy busy," said Jess. "It'll keep him out of trouble."

"I'll do that," agreed Reedy.

They finished eating and the horses were rested, so Jess put them into a run again, following the tracks. They continued a straight line, crossing a few little-used trails along the way.

It was getting later in the afternoon when Jess saw the grassy meadowland up ahead with a hill in the middle of it. He pointed it out to Reedy, who nodded.

"Let's ride close to the top, walk the rest of the way and see what's on the other side," said Jess.

They rode through the meadowland. When they reached the hill, they rode close to the top and dismounted. Jess took his spyglass and one of his buffalo rifles. He looked over at Reedy.

"Slide that other buffalo rifle out of the scabbard on Sharps," he said.

Reedy did and they walked up to the top of the hill. Getting down on their bellies, they both saw the prospector working the stream. He had a fire going close by.

"I wonder how long he's been down there," said Jess.

"Hard to know for sure without asking him."

Jess saw the forest down in the meadowland and extended his spyglass. He kept scanning the edge of it for a while, looking for any clues. He put the spyglass down and sighed.

"Those woods are too far away to see any detail, even with my spyglass."

"Well, it'll be dark in another hour or so," said Reedy.

"We've got no cover around us, so we might as well ride down to the bottom of the hill and eat a cold meal again."

"No hot coffee?" asked Reedy.

"Well, I've got some dried small branches tied to the back of the saddle on Sharps. We can make a tiny fire, just enough to brew some coffee."

"Okay then," said Reedy.

They walked back to the horses, put the rifles back in their scabbards and rode down the hill to the bottom and dismounted. Reedy took care of the horses and Jess made a tiny fire to brew coffee.

There was nowhere to string his cans around their perimeter, so they agreed to take turns at watch.

Reedy

Frank took the first watch, while Jess slept. Reedy sat Indian style, a Winchester in his hands.

He kept picturing Malone hanging from a rope.

CHAPTER TWENTY-FIVE

In the morning, Jess started a fire to brew coffee and warm up some beans with salt pork in them. After eating, they climbed up in the saddle and headed up the hill again. When they got close to the top, each took a buffalo rifle and walked the rest of the way up the hill.

Down on their bellies again, Jess scanned the trees to look for any evidence of fresh branches cut to make a path for horses. He saw the prospector cooking something on a fire while sipping what he figured was coffee.

"See any openings in those trees?" Reedy asked.

No, it's just too far away. I think we'll have to ride down there and walk along the tree line looking for any signs of one."

"What about the prospector?"

"Maybe we wait until he's pannin' the stream and we walk the horses down the hill as quietly as we can. We don't want him yelling out or taking a shot at us."

"Got any white cloth in those saddlebags?" Reedy asked.

Reedy

"Uh, yeah, in my medical kit."

"I'm going to the horses and get a strip of it you can tie to the end of your rifle as a show of peace to that prospector."

"All right," said Jess, "I'll come with you and we can ride the horses over the top and down the other side."

They went to the horses and Reedy got out the cloth from the medical kit. Jess tied it to the barrel of one of his Winchesters.

After climbing up in the saddle, they rode to the top of the hill. Once they stood on the top, Jess saw the tracks from Malone and his men as they had obviously stayed on the hill for a few minutes, looking at the forest below and deciding what to do.

Jess pointed to the tracks and Reedy nodded he understood. The prospector was still eating whatever he had cooked. His back was partially turned toward them, so he didn't see them approaching down the hill.

As they got closer, the prospector heard the creaking of leather. He slowly set his plate down, stood up and turned around to see two men with rifles. Both barrels were pointed up to the sky.

He saw the white strip of cloth tied to the end of the barrel of one of the rifles. When he saw the badge on Reedy's shirt, he relaxed a little. Jess and Reedy rode up to him.

Reedy had one of his index fingers to his lips, telling the prospector to be quiet. The two dismounted and walked to the man.

He looked at Reedy's badge again.

"How'd you get that hole in your badge?" he asked.

"Got shot and left for dead," Reedy told him.

"You must be lookin' fer someone, but it ain't me, 'cause I ain't done nothing wrong."

"We're lookin' for four men who we've been tracking," Reedy explained. "We're thinkin' they rode over that hill behind us and probably went inside those woods across the meadow."

"I ain't seen hide nor hair of anybody or anything out here, not even any gold or silver," he griped. "Found some back a mile or so upstream a month ago, but I've been working it slowly downstream for a few days now and got nuthin' to show for it."

"Are you going deep enough into the sediment?" Reedy asked.

"Yeah, as far as I can dig," he explained. "Even used a little shovel to dig deeper."

Jess looked at Reedy, his brow furrowed.

"Since when do you know about pannin' for gold and silver?" Jess asked him.

"I've worked at just about everything in my life," Reedy answered. "When I was a young boy, I worked at a general store. I used to fix damaged furniture for customers. Worked with leather, canvas, all sorts of cloth. I swear I always had a bruised thumb from hitting it with a hammer while tacking things down."

"Interesting," said Jess as he turned to the prospector.

"So, you haven't seen anyone or heard any gunshots since you got back here?"

"No, nuthin' like that."

"Well, listen," said Jess. "We're going to ride across the meadow to those trees and take a look-see. We'd like you to just go about your business and don't be staring at us in case they're in there and watching the meadow."

"Sure, anything to help the law," he said. "As long as I don't get shot."

Reedy put his hand on his shoulder.

"As long as you stay here and mind your own business, you'll be fine."

"All righty," he said.

Jess and Reedy mounted up again, crossed the stream and the meadow. Jess followed the tracks left in the soft soil. As they got closer, Jess scanned the edge of the trees and found what he was looking for. He glanced over at Reedy.

"I see where they entered those woods," he said quietly as he put the spyglass away. "I say we leave the horses here and go in on foot. Those woods are thick with trees and bushes."

"Okay," agreed Reedy.

"Stick some extra cartridges for that Winchester in your pockets and load the buffalo rifle with one of these," he said.

He handed Reedy the heavy-caliber cartridge from the pouch of cartridges, along with a handful of cartridges for the Winchester.

They dismounted and each of them carried a Winchester and a buffalo rifle. When they reached the opening to the woods, Jess saw the cut and broken branches on the trees to make an entrance to the dense forest. He pointed to the remnants of a few smokes on the ground, along with some used matchsticks.

"Someone has been coming out here and watching that hill and the meadow," he whispered to Reedy, who nodded.

Jess had the spyglass in his back pocket. He pulled it out and looked along the opened pathway. He put the spyglass away, sniffed the air and listened for any sounds. He didn't smell or hear anything.

"The opening goes in a long way," whispered Jess. "Let's go in slowly and stop often to listen for any noise or talking."

Reedy nodded and they slowly made their way along the passageway, one on the left side, one on the right. They had stopped a dozen times to listen and sniff the air for odors.

The next time they stopped, Reedy heard what sounded like a horse stomping his hoof on the ground. He put his hand up, looked over at Jess and touched his ear. Jess nodded that he'd heard it too.

He took his spyglass out again and kept scanning from left to right slowly, looking for any movement in the dense forest. He saw nothing.

They meticulously moved another ten yards and stopped. Jess scanned the area again, slowly and painstakingly with his spyglass.

Just before he was about to move ahead farther, he spotted the slightest movement between the trees. He moved closer to Reedy.

"I saw movement off to our right in that direction," he whispered as he pointed.

"We need to make certain it's them," he whispered back. "The last thing I want to do is kill some innocent hunters."

"Well, let's move another twenty feet or so and I'll scan again," whispered Jess.

Jess moved back to the other side of the opening and they walked slowly, heel to toe, watching for any twigs on the ground.

Suddenly, out of the woods came a huge buck, thrashing through the brush and trees, crossing in front of where Jess and Reedy stood, stone-still now.

In the clearing, all four men stood up and grabbed their rifles. They had heard the noise, but hadn't seen what made it. Vic Walker grabbed his field glasses and peered through them.

He didn't see any movement, but he saw the partial outline of what he thought was a man. He shot Malone a look.

"Someone has found us," he said in a soft voice. "You and Frenchy get to the escape path. Me and Tad will lay down cover fire."

Malone and Frenchy tightened the cinch straps on all four horses and Tad and Walker started firing their rifles in the general direction of where Jess and Reedy were, their backs against trees now to keep from taking a hot slug of lead.

Walker and Tad were firing in rotation. One would fire while the other was levering in another fresh round and then he would fire. That way, every second or so, a hot slug pounded the trees all around Jess and Reedy. Branches were being cut and bark flew off trees.

The intense fire slowed down when Tad took a few seconds to shove several fresh rounds into his rifle. Jess and Reedy both spun around and returned shots as fast as they could fire. Soon, the intense fire began again, forcing them to shove their backs against the tree trunks once more.

Meanwhile, Frenchy and Malone rode out of the clearing, following the zigzag pattern of the escape path. As soon as they hit the straight part, they heeled their horses into a dead run, leaning forward against their horses' necks to keep from being slapped with any branches.

Walker motioned for Tad to refill his rifle while he continued to fire. Once Tad's rifle was to full capacity, Walker fired his last bullet.

"Keep firing until you're empty and then make your escape," said Walker as he jumped on his horse and headed for the escape path.

Jess and Reedy both noticed the slower rate of fire. They returned fire in the general direction, even though they couldn't see their target.

Tad kept firing as he walked backward toward his horse. When the hammer clicked on an empty chamber, he jumped on his horse and gigged him to the escape path.

The firing stopped completely and Jess heard the beating of hooves. He grabbed one buffalo rifle and started moving quickly along the path.

Reedy

Reedy grabbed the other buffalo rifle and followed along with him. When they came into the clearing, they saw movement retreating. Jess quickly figured out the opening that was partially concealed by the zigzag passage.

He dropped the Winchester, ran across the clearing and through the right and left turns of the escape route. When he reached the straightaway, he lifted the sights on the buffalo rifle and propped the barrel of it on the stub of one of the cut branches.

He took aim at the retreating rider, who was almost three hundred yards out. Slowly he put pressure on the trigger until the rifle bucked and boomed against his shoulder.

The three-hundred-seventy-five-grain slug sizzled through the air. It slammed into Tad's back between his shoulder blades, exiting out his sternum, ripping his heart apart in the process.

He fell off one side of his horse, slammed into the ground and rammed into a tree trunk, breaking his backbone in half.

Reedy reached Jess as Tad's body hit the tree.

"Whoa, that had to hurt," he said.

Jess turned to him and pursed his lips.

"I don't think he felt that after the slug went through him," professed Jess.

"Well, let's go see who we got," said Reedy.

CHAPTER TWENTY-SIX

Jess and Reedy walked to the body and quickly realized it wasn't Ned Malone.

Reedy looked at the face and grunted.

"That's Tad," acknowledged Reedy. "Never used a last name for some reason."

"Malone was probably the first one out of that clearing," reasoned Jess. "Any reason we need to turn in this body?"

Reedy shook his head.

"No, we don't waste any time on this one here. We need to get after Malone as soon as we get back on the horses."

"Let's get our things, head to the horses, ride through this passageway and start tracking them again."

Leaving the body there, they walked back to the clearing, picked up the other rifles and walked out to the meadowland. The old prospector was standing up by the stream, looking in their direction.

After putting the rifles in their scabbards, they mounted up. Jess looked out at the prospector again and then at Reedy.

Reedy

"Let's go tell him to take whatever that man has on him of value and take his horse, who's probably on the other side of those woods, eating that thick grass."

"All right, but let's do it fast," said Reedy.

Jess started the horses in the direction of the prospector. When they reached him, he smiled nervously.

"I ain't heard that much gunfire since the war," exclaimed the prospector.

"Yeah, a lot of lead was flying," admitted Reedy.

The man looked at Reedy's badge again.

"You get shot again?"

Reedy shook his head.

"No, it's the same hole," he said as he tapped his badge.

"So, did you kill any of those men?"

"Yeah, said Jess. "Only one of 'em. His body is in the cleared escape path they made in the forest. You can go collect his things. Any money he has on him, his pistol and holster, his rifle, and his horse."

"You sure I can do that?"

"Anybody asks you about it, tell them Deputy Unites States Marshal Frank Reedy from Stratton gave you permission to do so. But no one is gonna question you about it anyway," explained Reedy. "That man was a murderous outlaw and didn't even have a last name. No one will miss him or his things."

"You want me to bury him?" the prospector asked.

Reedy and Jess both shrugged their shoulders indifferently.

"Don't do it for us," said Jess. "Critters gotta eat too."

The prospector looked at Jess and smiled slightly.

"I reckon they do, don't they," he said.

"Well, we gotta get moving," Reedy said.

Jess spun the horses around, catching Reedy off guard. He leaned to one side and held onto the saddle horn.

"You gotta warn me when you're gonna do that," he complained.

"Sorry," said Jess. "Sometimes I just forget."

Heading back to the forest, they rode into the opening and reached the clearing. Riding to the zigzag opening, they went through it and hit the straightaway path. Heading past the dead body, they continued along until they came out of the woods.

There was another large meadowland on this side. Jess looked at the tracks leading away and could tell the outlaws were riding fast. Extending his spyglass, he scanned the area ahead of them, but saw no evidence of the three who had gotten away.

"Don't see any of them," he said as he put the spyglass away.

Reedy pointed to the horse standing in the meadowland, munching on the lush grass.

"I don't think he's going anywhere for a while," he said as he looked at the stream that came out on this side of the forest. "He's got water and plenty to eat."

"It's gonna be dark in a few hours, so let's track them as far as we can before we make camp," suggested Jess.

"You're the tracker," grinned Reedy. "Lead the way."

Reedy

Jess started his horses again, but at a moderate gallop, due to the soft soil and tall grass. He kept his eyes moving from the tracks to the area ahead. Once they crossed out of the meadowland, he pushed the horses faster.

He wasn't sure if Malone and the two men he had left already had a spot in mind to hole up for the night.

Jess saw the sun starting its downward spiral. He slowed the horses to a walk and glanced at Reedy.

"We need to start looking for a spot with some cover to camp where we can have a fire," said Jess. "Not much daylight left now."

Reedy nodded. After resting the horses long enough, Jess put them into a fast gallop again. When Reedy spotted some trees that looked like they had been planted in rows, he waved his hand and then pointed to them.

Jess halted the horses, got out his spyglass and scanned the trees. He looked for any evidence of smoke coming from them, wondering if Malone and his men were holing up in there. He put the spyglass away and looked at Reedy.

"We'll approach those trees slowly in case Malone and the others are using them. Take the Winchester out and I'll pull out my buffalo rifle and load it. If they're in there, they'll start shooting too early and maybe I can get another one with the Sharps."

"Malone is smart and cagey," cautioned Reedy. "He'll wait till we're in range for his rifle before he shoots."

"Then maybe I'll fire off a few shots from five hundred yards out. There are only six rows of trees and they look like they were planted by someone to harvest for firewood."

"I don't see any house or cabin out there," advised Reedy.

"Maybe it burnt down or maybe it's on the other side of those trees."

"Yeah, maybe," admitted Reedy, acting warily.

When they reached a spot about five hundred yards out, Jess lifted the ladder sights and took aim at the trees. He felt the wind on his face. Calculating the distance, he aimed higher and fired the heavy-caliber rifle.

He looked up and saw one of the trees shake slightly when the slug slammed into it, knocking branches and leaves to the ground. He peered through the spyglass and saw nothing, no movement. No fire came back. He handed Reedy the spyglass.

"I'm gonna fire again," Jess told him as he chambered a fresh round. "Watch through the spyglass and look for any movement."

"Okay," Reedy said as he put the end of the spyglass to his eye.

"Jeez, this is the most powerful spyglass or scope I've ever looked through before."

"It can see farther and more clearly than any other one I've ever looked through," agreed Jess.

He raised the rifle and fired again, this time several feet to one side of where he'd fired the first time. No movement or return fire. Jess reloaded the Sharps rifle and put it back in

Reedy

the scabbard. Sliding out his Winchester, he levered a round into it and released the hammer.

"Let's approach slowly and keep your eyes peeled," said Jess.

Walking the horses toward the trees, they finally saw the remnants of what was obviously a very old sod house. It had fallen and slumped into a pile of grass and dirt from many rainfalls.

"Now we know who planted those trees," declared Reedy.

"We're within range of a rifle, so if they're in there, they're waiting to ambush us when we get closer, so be alert," said Jess.

When they rode into the trees, they found an old camp that someone had used a long time ago. Jess scanned all through the trees and saw nothing to worry about.

"I think we can camp here tonight and light out in the morning," said Jess as he slid his rifle back into its scabbard and dismounted. "Why don't you get a fire going and I'll take care of the horses and set my cans out so we can both sleep through the night."

Reedy nodded and went around picking up dead branches. He got a fire going. Jess strung his cans around their perimeter and Reedy started cooking a pan of potted meat and sliced potatoes. He added a can of corn to it.

After eating, Jess brewed some Arbuckles' and they sipped coffee until darkness settled in. Jess poured a little water from a canteen to douse the fire.

"Well, we had a hot meal and some coffee," said Reedy. "We can hit the trail hard in the morning again."

"I wonder how far Malone got ahead of us," Jess pondered out loud.

"You never know with Malone," advised Reedy. "He's escaped custody more than any other criminal I know of."

"Well, he won't escape us, no matter how long it takes," Jess assured him.

"Oh, and if you get another one of 'em in your sights, make sure it ain't Malone, 'cause Judge Hood will be pissed if he doesn't get to hang him personally," said Reedy. "And just so we're clear about it, that's an order."

"Yes, sir," Jess said, grinning.

"I'm really serious about it," said Reedy. "I was relieved when I saw it wasn't Malone you killed back in those woods."

"I hear ya, but if it comes down to a choice of either me or you dying by Malone's hands, all bets are off," said Jess.

"Fair enough," he said. "But only if it's a choice of one of us or him, and then, try to wound him if you can and I'll do the same."

"That works for me," Jess assured him. "Now, let's get some much-needed rest."

They crawled into their bedrolls and fell off to a light sleep.

CHAPTER TWENTY-SEVEN

Malone, Walker and Frenchy were pushing their horses to their limits. When they finally had to slow them down to rest for the third time, the sun was heading down. Walker looked over at Malone after turning in the saddle again to see their back trail.

"Either Tad didn't follow us or he got himself killed," reasoned Walker.

"There was that one last shot as we were clearing that meadowland area," said Frenchy.

"Well, we can't worry about it now," said Malone. "We're gonna walk the horses all through the night again."

"Who do you think tried to attack us back in those woods?" Frenchy asked.

"Well, we killed one of the top Deputy United States Marshals, Frank Reedy," professed Walker. "My guess is they sent more U.S. Marshals after us. If they catch us, they'll probably hang us from the nearest tree or anything they can find tall enough to string a rope over."

"Well, whoever it was, we ain't gettin' caught," declared Malone.

"You got another place in mind to hide out again?" Walker asked.

"First, let's ride through the night and eat in the saddle," explained Malone. "There are two spots I can think of, depending on how far we can travel tonight and tomorrow."

"All right," said Walker.

They rode through the entire night, riding in single file. As soon as the sun started shedding light over the landscape, they started running the horses fast again.

Before the noon hour, the landscape changed from sparse grass and flatland to a rocky landscape with small hills here and there. Malone reined his horse in and gazed behind him at the other two, who looked confused.

"Why are we slowin' down?" Frenchy asked.

"We'll walk the horses for several miles over this rocky ground," Malone explained. "That way, whoever is tracking us will have a much harder time following."

"How do you figure?" asked Walker.

"Running across this hard rocky ground will crush more pebbles and stones," explained Malone. "By walking the horses, they won't break as many stones or make as many scratches in the rocky ground."

"That's smart thinkin'," boss," said Frenchy.

"How do you think I've escaped so many times before. Now,

Reedy

spread out and ride abreast. If we ride single file, we increase the odds of crushing more stones and pebbles."

They spread out, riding abreast and apart from one another. They walked the horses for about three miles or so and then Malone looked over at them.

"Let's push 'em hard again, boys," he said.

They gigged their horses into a gallop again. Malone felt confident that would throw anyone following them off their tracks.

What he didn't know was…who was tracking him.

***

Reedy stirred when his nose caught the smell of bacon cooking. He got up on his elbows and saw Jess frying it in the pan.

He looked over at Reedy and smiled.

"About time you got up," said Jess.

Reedy sat up and yawned.

"I'm not used to being out on the trail all the time like you," he said as he stretched.

"I'll bet you miss that nice hotel bed back at the Stratton Hotel."

"It's a little more comfortable than sleeping on cold hard ground."

"Yeah, I agree with that," Jess said as he forked out the bacon and poured pan bread mixture into the grease.

He put a few slices of bacon on a plate and handed it to

Reedy, who took it and stood up. He put nuts, raisins, and some cut-up apple chunks into the mixture and cooked it slowly.

After eating the bacon and pan bread, Jess made coffee. When they had finished and cleaned up, they mounted up, headed out of the trees and returned to the spot where Malone and his men had left tracks.

They followed them for a while and suddenly Jess put his hands up and halted the horses. He dismounted and began walking behind his horses. Reedy turned in the saddle.

"What is it?" he asked.

"Give me a minute," he said as he kept walking slowly along the tracks.

He bent down and examined them several times. He finally stood up and walked back to the horses. He swung back up on Gray.

"They were running their horses when they left the hideout in the forest," he explained. "But what the tracks are telling me now is they never made camp. Instead, they walked their horses through the night."

"You sure?" Reedy asked.

"I'll bet these tracks don't veer off to any camp they used last night."

"Well, like I told ya, Malone is smart and cagey."

"Maybe, but he's not going to outsmart me."

Jess put the horses into a gallop again. They saw there was no veering off the tracks, telling them Malone and his men rode through the night and never made camp.

Reedy

They reached the spot where the three outlaws started running their horses again. Jess halted the horses to get down and examine them closer. He looked up at Reedy.

"This is where they started the horses fast again when daylight hit."

"They wanted to put some distance between them and us," advised Reedy.

"Yeah, but we can eventually make up the difference with my horses. They've been riding pretty much in a straight line since they left you for dead. Any idea where they might be headed?"

"No, not really, admitted Reedy.

Jess took out the map of the area and studied it. He saw the town of Burlington up ahead.

"Ever been to the town of Burlington?" Jess asked.

"Only a few times. Small town. No law."

"Does Malone have any reason to go there?"

Reedy shook his head.

"None that I can think of, except for supplies or whiskey, but only if they needed them."

"Well, it's not too far off the direction that they seem to be staying in," said Jess.

"Do you think we'd reach Burlington before dark?"

"Could, if we keep pushing the horses hard and eat cold in the saddle."

"I'll trade that for a soft bed for the night," admitted Reedy.

Jess put the map away and climbed up in the saddle. He started the horses again. They rode for a while and when they hit the rocky terrain, Jess put his hand up and signified he was stopping the horses again.

"What now?" Reedy asked as Jess slid from the saddle.

"I lost the tracks," said Jess.

"Are you serious?"

"Let me look around for a minute."

Jess walked along the area up ahead, bending down several times. He picked up several pebbles. He looked over at Reedy, who was watching him with interest.

"I can still track 'em," advised Jess. "He's smart though, no doubt about that. Even though they're riding abreast now and walking the horses, I can still find freshly busted pebbles and stones, still heading in the same direction."

Jess walked back to Gray and climbed up in the saddle. He took out his spyglass and scanned the area ahead of them. He put it away and looked over at Reedy.

"My guess is they'll walk the horses for a while and then start them running again."

"You've really got this tracking business down, huh?"

"Frank, the ground tells a story, as long as you watch and listen to it long enough."

They started the horses again. Jess stopped frequently to examine the ground. After a while, he pointed to the scrapings in the rocky terrain.

"This is where they stopped walking the horses and put them into a gallop again," explained Jess.

"How far are we from Burlington?" Reedy asked.

Reedy

"By my calculations, we could reach it in two more hours, just before dark. If they continue in the same direction, they would only be a few miles out from the town."

When they reached the spot on the little-used trail that veered off to the town of Burlington, Malone and his men continued in the same direction.

Jess stopped the horses.

"They didn't go to the town, so they must not need supplies yet," he said.

"That, or they have someplace particular in mind they're heading to."

"Is there a hotel in this town?"

Reedy shook his head.

"No, but Bud's Saloon has good rooms and food," explained Reedy.

"You've been there before?"

"Yeah, Bud's an old friend of mine from when I worked as a deputy town marshal in my early days. "He's a good cook. Only cooks one thing a night, but it's always good."

"Okay then, let's go get a hot meal and a soft bed," said Jess. "We'll come back here in the morning and continue tracking 'em."

They rode into the sleepy little town of Burlington. Stopping at the town livery, they slid from the saddle and Jess walked the horses inside.

"Anyone working in here?" Reedy called out.

There was no answer.

"Well, let's take care of the horses ourselves and head to the saloon," said Jess.

When they finished, they each took a rifle and headed out of the livery. They walked to the saloon. Not a person was out and about and most of the few businesses were closed.

When they walked into the saloon, Bud was delivering a bowl of food to one of the few customers he had in the place. He smiled at Reedy as he set the food down in front of the man.

"Marshal Frank Reedy," he said cheerily. "Been a long time since you've been back this way."

Reedy walked up to him and shook his hand.

Bud noticed the hole in the badge and the dried blood on the shirt.

"What the heck happened?" he asked.

"Long story, but I'm gonna live," he answered.

Bud looked at Jess.

"I know this man, but I'm surprised you're riding with him," said Bud.

"He's a good friend and an excellent tracker," explained Reedy. "We're on the trail of Ned Malone."

"He's on the loose again?" asked Bud.

"Yeah, and it's my fault," admitted Reedy. "I was escorting him to Calico when some of his men ambushed us. They left me for dead, but I was only slightly wounded."

"I've got a pot of beef stew on the stove and it's really good," said Bud. "I'll get you two a bowl and something to drink. I suppose you want rooms too?"

Reedy

"Yeah, just for the night," said Reedy.

They sat at a table. Bud brought out bowls of the stew and freshly baked bread with butter. After two helpings each, they retired to their rooms for the night and fell off to sleep.

CHAPTER TWENTY-EIGHT

The next morning found Reedy and Jess eating a morning meal in Bud's Saloon. Jess finished first. He stood up, donned his hat and grabbed his Winchester.

"You go ahead and finish up," said Jess. "I'm gonna get the horses ready."

"I'll be along in a few minutes," said Reedy as he looked over at Bud, who was serving another table.

"Bud, I need another cup of coffee and one more of those biscuits," Reedy told him.

"Just took another batch out of the oven," said Bud. "Nice and hot."

"That's the way I like 'em," said Reedy.

Bud went back to the kitchen and Reedy was taking another sip of his coffee when he saw a man riding up in front of the saloon. He slowly put his cup down and reached below the table.

Slipping his hammer strap off, he slid his gun out of his holster, thumbed the hammer back all the way and waited.

Reedy

Ezra Windom was a ruthless bank robber and killer that Reedy had caught and sent to the state penitentiary many years ago. He was older and haggard-looking now, but Reedy would never forget that face or the threat he had made.

Windom dismounted, slipped his hammer strap off and took the steps up to the batwings. He pushed through them and stood there, looking around at the men inside.

His eyes finally stopped when he saw the familiar face of the man sitting at the table in the corner. His eyes narrowed and his face took on an angry expression as he realized who it was.

"Frank Reedy?" he asked in a gruff voice.

Reedy kept the gun pointed at Window under the table.

"Who let your sorry ass out of prison?" Reedy asked.

"I'm sure you had nothin' to do with it," he grumbled hatefully.

"That's for sure," said Reedy. "If it were up to me, you'd have died of old age in that cell."

"You took a whole lot of years of my life away."

"You did that all by yourself, Windom. Killing that bank manager on your last job was what got you that time, and that was a light sentence as far as I'm concerned."

"You remember the last thing I told you when you turned me over to the guards at the penitentiary?"

"Yeah, word for word. You said that the next time you laid eyes on me, you'd kill me, and it was a promise, not a threat."

Windom moved his right hand down by the butt of his gun. He sneered at Reedy, hate spilling from his narrowed eyes.

"I wasn't lookin' for ya, but now that I found ya, I'm gonna make good on that promise, even if it sends me back to that hellhole you put me in."

Windom went for his gun, but he never got it halfway out of the holster. Reedy fired his gun from under the table. The slug from Reedy's pistol rammed into Windom's hip, just below his gun belt.

Reedy stood up as Windom stumbled backward toward the batwings. He fanned two more shots. The slugs hit Windom in the right and left sides of his chest.

His upper torso twisted one way and then another as he continued stumbling backward. His legs started to give out and he fell through the batwing doors.

Jess was still in the livery when he heard the first shot. He grabbed his Colt from the front of his holster and rushed out of the livery just in time to see a man's body flying through the batwing doors of Bud's Saloon.

The body landed on the steps of the front porch. His feet were resting on the top step, and his head was on the ground. His neck was bent so that his chin was pushed into his chest.

His gun had fallen out of the holster when he crashed through the batwings. It landed in the dirt off to one side of the body.

Jess stood there and Reedy walked out of the saloon with his gun in one hand and a biscuit in the other. He took a bite from the biscuit and chewed.

Jess slowly walked over to where the body lay, stretched out on the steps. He tucked the Colt back into the front of his holster and sighed as he looked up at Reedy, chewing on the biscuit.

"Now who can't be left alone for a short time without killing someone?" Jess asked in a sarcastic tone.

Reedy swallowed and grunted.

"That's Ezra Windom. I put him in prison many years ago. I reckon he had a beef with me, but that's over with now."

"I can plainly see that."

Reedy held up the biscuit.

"Fresh out of the oven," said Reedy. "You want one?"

"Wrap one in a napkin and I'll eat it later. I'll bring the horses here while you finish up."

Reedy popped the biscuit into his mouth and held it there while he replaced the spent shells in his pistol and holstered it. He walked back into the saloon as a few men stepped outside to look at the body.

Jess brought the two horses out of the livery and over to the saloon. The body had already been moved to the side of the saloon. Reedy walked out and had a napkin with two fresh biscuits wrapped in it. He handed it to Jess, who put it in his saddlebags.

"There's two in there and one of 'em is mine," advised Reedy as he climbed up in the saddle on Sharps.

Jess climbed up on Gray and grinned at Reedy.

"Anyone else in town you need to kill before we leave?"

"Nope, don't think so," he said as he looked around.

"All right then, let's get back on the hunt for Malone."

They rode out of town and back to where they had left off last night. Jess found the tracks again and they continued following them.

***

Ned Malone, Vic Walker and Frenchy had finally made camp and took turns at watch for the night. The next day, they were heading along a trail that was narrow and had not been used in quite some time.

They were stopped at a shallow river, letting the horses drink and munch on some of the lush grass on the edge of it. Frenchy was turned in the saddle, watching their back trail.

Walker turned to Malone, who seemed to be deep in thought.

"So, where are we headed, boss?" he asked.

Malone jerked his head, breaking his thoughts.

"Oh, uh…I think we're gonna go to the town of Woodburn."

"But…that town's been dead for years now," said Walker.

Frenchy heard the name and looked over at Malone.

"Did you say Woodburn?" he asked.

"Yeah," answered Malone.

"Why would we want to go there?" asked Frenchy.

"I'm gettin' tired of always runnin' from the law," answered Malone. "I say we go there and make a stand with whoever is chasing our tail. We'll have the advantage of surprise and we can be ready for them when they arrive, whoever it is."

"But we don't know how many men are behind us," explained Walker. "It could be a posse of a dozen or more."

"Maybe, but most likely the majority of 'em will be volunteers who don't have experience like we do. If we do this right, we could take down four or five before they even know what happened. We can reinforce our positions and be ready when they arrive."

Walker hung his head and sighed. He picked his head up and looked over at Frenchy, who just shrugged his shoulders indifferently. He looked back over at Malone.

"Boss, I think we got a pretty good head start on whoever is following us," declared Walker. "I say we keep going. Maybe ride through another night again to get even more of a lead."

Malone looked over at Walker.

"Vic, I've been in and out of prisons and jails most of my adult life. I can't keep runnin' forever. I'll understand if you don't want to make a stand. If you want to split off and go your own way, I won't object. It's me they want so badly after killing that judge's wife. They'll never stop hunting for me and I'd rather die in a shootout than let that judge hang me in front of a bunch of strangers."

Walker hung his head again and sighed. He lifted it and looked at Malone.

"We've been friends too long for me to abandon you now," said Walker. "If you want to make a stand of it, I'm gonna be right with you."

"Me too," added Frenchy.

"Okay then, let's go set ourselves up for a battle," said Malone.

They crossed the river and headed along the trail that would eventually take them to the abandoned town of Woodburn.

CHAPTER TWENTY-NINE

Malone and his men finally reached the dilapidated and abandoned town late in the afternoon. They took their horses to the livery to see if anything was left there.

To their surprise, they found bales of hay in the hayloft and a few bags of oats on a work counter. After taking care of their horses, they took their rifles and saddlebags to the saloon on the only street in town.

The batwings squeaked loudly when they opened them. After walking in and looking around the cobweb-infested saloon, they found several half empty bottles of cheap rotgut and a few full ones. Malone looked at the other two.

"Take a walk around town and see if you can find any guns or ammo left," said Malone.

"Sure thing, boss," said Frenchy.

Walker and Frenchy walked out and headed in different directions. Walker went to the general store first. It was mostly empty, but he did find some canned goods and luckily, two boxes of .44-40 rifle cartridges.

He loaded the canned goods in a wooden crate, along with the rifle cartridges. He carried them to the saloon and set the crate on one of the tables.

"Two boxes of rifle cartridges and a dozen or so cans of food," said Walker.

"I found some canned goods in the back along with flour, salt, cornmeal and a few other things," said Malone.

Frenchy walked in carrying a sack of stuff.

"What did you find?" Walker asked.

"Cans of corned beef, some cans of beans and a bag of jerky," said Frenchy.

"Well, we've got enough to eat for a week then, and plenty of ammo, especially with what we have in our saddlebags," explained Malone. "There's plenty of wood in the kitchen for the cookstove and some pans left too."

"How 'bout water?" Walker asked.

"There's a well pump in the kitchen at the sink and I spotted one out behind the saloon by the privy," answered Malone.

"Well, as late as it is in the afternoon, I don't think whoever is trailing us will arrive today," reasoned Walker. "Maybe we can eat a nice hot meal and start gettin' ready tomorrow?"

"I think that's safe to say," agreed Malone. "But to be on the safe side, we'll put our rifles in three locations with extra cartridges next to them. Walker, tomorrow you go to the top floor of the livery. You should be able to see anyone coming in from either end early enough to be ready for them. Put a man in your sights, but don't shoot till I do, understand? Frenchy, you take the field glasses, get on the roof of the saloon and keep watch."

Both men nodded they understood. Frenchy went about starting a fire in the stove to cook a meal. Walker and Malone set the fully loaded rifles out with a box of cartridges for each one.

After eating supper, they rolled their bedrolls out on the saloon floor. Malone and Walker crawled into theirs and fell off to sleep. Malone took first watch, sitting at a table by the front window of the saloon, watching and waiting.

***

Jess and Reedy rode all through the day. They came across the camp that had been used by Malone and his men. They sat in the saddle, looking around their camp.

"They must have ridden through the night again to get this far to make camp," calculated Jess. They must be gettin' tired of runnin' by now."

"That would be my guess too," agreed Reedy. "We'd best be wary of ambush spots now."

"I'm always watching for ambush spots, Frank, all the time," offered Jess.

"I should've figured that with you."

Jess took out his map of the area and studied it again.

"Well, there ain't nothing for the next few days' ride from here, except for Woodburn," acknowledged Jess. "It's been abandoned for years though."

Reedy lowered his head in thought, thinking about everything he knew about Malone. He slowly lifted his head and looked over at Jess, who was still studying the map.

"You know what?" Reedy asked.

Jess looked up at him questioningly.

"What's on your mind, Frank?"

Frank grinned knowingly.

"Woodburn is on my mind."

"You think they'll go there, thinking we won't because it's abandoned?"

"That's the kind of move Malone would make, being as cagey as he is."

Jess looked at the map again.

"Woodburn ain't that far off the trail we've been following," he said. "Besides, if their tracks turn toward Woodburn, we'll follow them wherever they lead us."

"We can make camp tonight and should be able to reach Woodburn by noon tomorrow," said Reedy.

Jess folded the map and put it away.

"Let's go then," said Jess as he started the horses out to the trail again.

They rode for the remainder of the day, stopping occasionally for Jess to examine the tracks closer. He was looking to see if one of the horses had separated from the others.

It was another calculated guess they made, wondering if Malone would split off from the other two to escape capture yet again.

Reedy

Before the sun went too far down over the horizon, they found a suitable place to make camp for the night. Reedy made a simple meal of fried potatoes with chopped pieces of salt pork mixed in with it.

Jess made pan bread, adding a lot of raisins and blueberries. They ate the bread with coffee. He had mashed some of the blueberries into the batter, and added some sugar for flavor and color.

"You've gotten pretty good at making this pan bread," admitted Reedy. "This almost tastes like a dessert."

"I've learned to make it several different ways, depending on what I have available. Sometimes it's plain, sometimes it's finely cut-up potatoes with bacon or salt pork and sometimes it's like this, with fruits and sugar added. Whenever I come across an apple tree or some fruit bushes, like berries, I stop and pick some."

They finished eating and turned in for the night.

***

Malone and the two others woke at the first signs of daylight. They ate first and then went about setting up their positions to make a stand with whoever was trailing them.

Malone set himself up in the saloon. His rifle was fully loaded. He went to the two front windows and broke out the remaining glass to be able to shoot without anything in the way.

He put tables against the wall under each of the two front windows for extra protection and left a pile of extra cartridges on the floor under them.

In the back kitchen of the saloon, he put a table top against the wall of the one window there, along with extra cartridges. He locked the back door and put a chair under the knob.

Frenchy was on top of the two-story saloon, with a good view of both ends of the street. He had put extra cartridges at both sides of the parapet. He had the field glasses with him, peering at both entrances to the town.

Walker went to the livery and climbed the ladder to the hayloft. There was a window on the front, one on the side facing one entrance to the town and one in the back.

He put extra shells below each window and stacked up bales of hay against the wall below the window. He set one bale of hay on the floor to sit on.

Back in the saloon, Malone walked out the back door and up the steps to the roof, where Frenchy was peering through the field glasses. He lowered them when he heard Malone coming up the steps.

"See anything yet?" asked Malone.

"Just some rolling sagebrush and a few rabbits," he answered. "We kept a pretty good lead on whoever was chasing us, so I don't 'spect to see anyone till later in the afternoon."

"You're probably right," agreed Malone. "I'm gonna make some soup down in the kitchen out of what we have. We can take turns eating later in the day."

"I just hope it's mostly a volunteer posse after us," declared Frenchy. "I'd hate to exchange lead with a bunch of them federal marshals. They's a tough bunch of hombres for sure."

Reedy

"Yeah, well, there's one less of 'em now," said Malone.

Frenchy looked at him and grinned.

"You really enjoyed plugging that Reedy fella, didn't ya?"

"Even more than I did strangling that judge's wife," he admitted before heading down the steps again.

CHAPTER THIRTY

Reedy and Jess broke camp in the morning. They continued to follow the tracks left by Malone and his two men. When they were only a few miles away from the abandoned town of Woodburn, Jess halted the horses and looked at where the tracks veered off toward the town.

"What is it?" Reedy asked.

"Well, their tracks are heading along this almost nonexistent trail leading toward the town of Woodburn."

"Are you sure?"

"Absolutely."

Reedy sat in the saddle, thinking about Malone.

"Why do you think they went there?"

Jess shrugged his shoulders.

"There's nothing there," he said. "It's been vacant for almost ten years now."

"Does it look like they tried to cover their tracks?"

Jess moved the horses along the overgrown trail for a few hundred feet, looking down at the tracks. He shook his head.

"No, the tracks are still plainly visible."

"Maybe they just wanted to sleep under a roof for a night?" Reedy pondered.

"Could be, but if they wanted to throw us off, they should have tried to cover their tracks somehow."

"Malone is too smart to make a simple mistake like that," said Reedy. "He didn't cover his tracks for a reason. Either he and his men just wanted to sleep under a roof for a night and keep going or he wants us to find him there."

"You think maybe he wants to make a last stand of it?"

"I've known Malone for a long time. He never does anything without a reason. He does not want to die at the end of a rope with strangers watching. He'd rather go out in a hail of gunfire instead."

"Well, his two men, whoever they are, are sticking with him, unless they just rode to Woodburn with him and left him there to make his last stand."

Reedy shook his head.

"No, his men are committed to him. You saw that back at that forest. He sacrificed one man so he and the other two had a chance to escape. He's done it before."

"All right then. We have to go on the assumption that they're waiting for whoever is chasing them to show up and ambush them."

"Which means we have to proceed with the utmost caution," advised Reedy.

"Assuming they'll be watching from a rooftop, we have to find the best way to get into the town without being seen."

"Let's get close enough for you to look around with that spyglass of yours. Maybe you can figure out where they are in town. If I know Malone, and I do, he'll have his men spread out, so they'll be firing from three different positions."

"What if he had more men waiting there for him? That may be why he's continued in the same direction all this time."

"That's possible," Reedy admitted.

"Well, we're not far from Woodburn, so let's proceed slowly and watch for any traps they might have set for us. Like ropes tied across the trail or holes in the ground. We'll go slowly and when we get close to town, we'll go in on foot and get a good look at what we're dealing with."

"All right," said Reedy.

They proceeded very slowly, looking for any traps that might have been set for them. As soon as Jess spotted the town, he stopped the horses. He got his spyglass out and scanned the buildings from quite a distance.

"See anything yet?" Reedy asked.

"Not yet, but we're still quite far out. I see a wooded area we can leave the horses in and work our way toward the town to get a closer view."

"Lead the way," said Reedy.

They worked their way to the stand of trees on one side of the town's only street. They dismounted. Jess took both his Winchester and his Sharps buffalo rifle out of the scabbards on Gray.

Reedy

He grabbed the pouch of cartridges and threw it over his shoulder. He looked over at Reedy, who was sliding the Winchester out on Sharps.

"Frank, bring a canteen and some jerky," he said. "Just take the Winchester this time. I've got plenty of shells for it."

Reedy nodded, threw a canteen over his shoulder and got out a bag of venison jerky. Jess started walking through the trees until they came close to the edge facing the backs of the buildings in town.

Jess leaned the buffalo rifle against a tree and began searching the buildings, looking for any movement.

The backs of the buildings were about nine hundred feet away and the back of the saloon was easily visible through the spyglass. He kept his gaze focused on the roof of the saloon for a long time.

"Nothing yet?" Reedy asked.

"No, if anyone is on the roof of the saloon, he's sitting down and in front, out of sight from here. The livery is on the other side of the street and I can see the top of it but not the windows. Those are the two most likely places Malone would put his men to watch for anyone approaching the town."

On the roof of the saloon, Frenchy was sitting against the inside of the front façade, smoking a thin cheroot. When he finished, he threw it away, slowly stood up again and peered through the field glasses. Jess saw him.

"Okay, one man on the roof of the saloon with field glasses," said Jess. "He's looking around in all directions, so don't make any sudden movements."

Frenchy looked in all four directions and saw nothing. Inside the saloon, Malone was moving from the front windows to the back window of the saloon, watching for anyone approaching.

He had a large pot of soup on the stove, simmering slowly. Whenever he came to look out the back window, he stirred it. Jess saw a slight wisp of smoke rising out of the metal stack coming out the back wall of the saloon.

"I see a little bit of smoke coming out from the stove inside," said Jess.

"I'm bettin' that's where Malone is," said Reedy. "He'll be in the most protected spot and put his men out as lookouts."

"Wait a second," said Jess as he saw movement by the back window of the saloon.

"What do you see?"

"Well, it's still quite far from here, but I think Malone just peeked out through the back window of the kitchen in the saloon."

"That accounts for two men, so where is the third?"

Jess put the spyglass down and looked at Reedy. Then, he looked up at the tree they were standing next to. Jess started removing all his weapons and his hat.

"What are you gonna do?" Reedy asked.

"Do you want to climb up this tree?" Jess asked him.

"At my age? Are you nuts?"

"That's what I thought, especially at your age," Jess said, grinning.

Reedy frowned at him.

"I'm still your boss."

"What? You gonna fire me?"

"Well…no."

"I didn't think so…boss."

"Git your ass up that tree and find out where that third man is."

Jess put the spyglass in his back pocket.

"Give me a boost," Jess told him.

Reedy intertwined his fingers and Jess put his boot in them. Reedy grunted and hoisted him up to the first branch of the tree. Jess went very slowly, stopping every time he went up to the next branch.

When he was high enough to see all the rooftops, he got the spyglass out and peered through it. He watched the livery for a long time and then he saw a face appear in the front window of the hayloft.

"There you are," he whispered to himself.

He made his way to the bottom of the tree and hung on the last branch. He let go and landed on his feet, bending at the knees to absorb the shock.

"Well?" Reedy asked.

"The third man is in the hayloft of the livery, just like I figured."

"So, what's the plan?"

"It's over nine hundred feet to the roof of the saloon, so I'll have to shoot him with my buffalo rifle. A Winchester might miss from that distance and even if I hit him, it might not kill him. Then we'd have a wounded and angry man to deal with. My fifty-caliber slugs don't wound very often. Even if I hit an arm or leg, the slug will most likely sever a main artery and he'll bleed out."

"You have to make sure it's not Malone on the roof. We want Malone alive."

"Does Malone have long black hair?"

"No, his hair is a sandy color."

"The man on the roof of the saloon has long black hair and wears his gun on his left hip."

"Then that's not Malone. He wears his gun on his right leg."

"I'll kill the man on the roof tomorrow."

"Why tomorrow?"

"They're probably thinkin' whoever is chasing them will arrive today. If we wait until tomorrow, they might get a little more relaxed. I don't think they're going anywhere either, because they'd have left in the morning."

"Then, let's go back to the horses and make something to eat before the sun goes down."

"I'll put up a blanket to hide the fire, although I don't think they'd see it from this distance and through all the cover of trees."

"All right then," said Reedy as they headed back to where they had left the horses.

CHAPTER THIRTY-ONE

Jess put up a blanket to help cover the small fire they made. After a simple meal of bacon and beans, they sipped coffee.

Reedy looked over at Jess, who was gazing into the glowing embers of the fire.

"What are ya thinkin', Jess?"

He looked up at Reedy.

"Well, I was wondering if I should make my way around town and try to kill the man at the livery first."

"Why?"

"Well, the saloon is an easy shot from here, but once I take it, the man at the livery will be very guarded."

"I see your point, but if you're all the way over there, and I'm here, you might be stuck staying there until dark. And I can't get your horses moving without you. I say we should stay together. The other two might make a run for it and I won't be able to do anything until you get back here. I can shoot your other buffalo rifle, but I'm not an expert shot like you."

"I also thought about going in at night, but they'll hear the first shot and the other two will hunker down. Plus, with the fact that I can't kill Malone, it makes it more difficult to see who I'm shootin' at in the dark."

"Looks like we gotta go with your first idea, shooting the man on the roof of the saloon, provided Malone doesn't take turns on the roof," said Reedy.

"Yeah, I agree," sighed Jess.

"Well, I'll take first watch and hope we have some luck tomorrow," said Reedy.

Jess took the blanket down after dousing the fire. He crawled into his bedroll and lay there, thinking about the plan for tomorrow.

Back in the saloon, an hour after dark, Frenchy came down from the roof to the back door of the saloon, whistling to let Malone know it was him. Malone had two oil lamps burning on their lowest setting and on the floor to keep the slightest bit of light so they could move around.

He put one on the floor behind the bar and one in the kitchen on the floor behind the cookstove. Malone unlocked the back door and removed the chair.

Frenchy walked in and smelled the soup.

"I'm starvin'," he said.

"Get some soup and eat," said Malone as he locked the door again and put the chair under the knob again.

"Did Vic come back yet?" Frenchy asked as he ladled soup into a bowl.

"Not yet, but I expect him soon."

Malone walked to the front part of the saloon, carrying his rifle with him. He sat down at a table by the front window, staying in the shadows of the corner.

He heard the familiar whistle, letting him know that Walker was coming in. A few seconds later, he came slowly through the squeaking batwings.

"Don't shoot; it's just me," he said. "I smell something cooking."

Frenchy came out of the kitchen with a bowl of soup.

"Pot is on the stove," he told Walker.

Walker went to the kitchen and returned with a bowl. He sat down at the same table with Frenchy and Malone.

"Either of you see anything out there?" Malone asked.

"Nope, nuthin' but rolling sage brushes and rabbits," said Walker.

"Same here," agreed Frenchy. "I wanted to shoot a few of 'em, but figured it wouldn't be a good idea."

"No, it wouldn't," said Malone.

"Do you think it's possible the posse chasing us decided to not come here because it's an abandoned town?" asked Walker.

"Not if they have a decent tracker," said Malone. "They found our hideout in that forest, so I'm thinkin' they have a good one."

"This soup needs more meat in it," said Frenchy.

"Well, we don't have more meat," said Malone. "I used half the jerky in that soup and saved the other half for the next batch."

"I'll take first watch tonight," offered Frenchy.

Malone nodded.

"Vic, you take second watch and I'll take the last," he said. Frenchy, keep the cookstove warm for the soup."

"Yes, sir," he said as some of the soup ran down his chin.

They finished eating. Frenchy went to the stove and put a few small pieces of wood into it. Malone and Walker got into their bedrolls and fell off to sleep.

***

Jess had put the blanket up again to hide the fire, even though Malone and his men couldn't see it this far into the trees.

Reedy was eating the last of the pan bread and sipping coffee. He looked up at Jess, who was checking over his buffalo rifle.

"You gonna shoot the man standing guard on the roof of the saloon today?"

Jess nodded.

"Yeah, but not until later in the afternoon," he explained. "I want them to think no one is coming for them. I have an idea though."

"What is it?"

"Why don't you work yourself as close to the end of the street where the livery is. Stay in the cover so you're not seen by the man at the livery. Once I'm sure it's not Malone on the roof, I'll take the shot. When that happens, the man in the livery will be focusing on the saloon. That might give you enough time to make your way to the building across from the livery. I'm guessing it's not Malone up there, so that means we could have two of them out of the fray and only have to deal with Malone in the saloon."

Reedy sat there, thinking about the idea. He finally looked up at Jess.

"The only thing I worry about is that the man in the livery might just jump on his horse, take Malone's horse to the front of the saloon and make a run for it. I'm sure they're leaving the horses saddled and ready to ride at a moment's notice."

"Based on the fact that he's staying in the saloon and hasn't made any attempt to escape yet, I think Malone's done runnin'," stated Jess.

"I gotta admit, I think that too."

"Let's wait until the noon hour and then we make our move."

"Just don't kill Malone unless there's no other alternative."

"I'll do my best," said Jess.

After a while, they went to the spot close to the edge of the trees. Taking his spyglass out, Jess peered through it and saw it was the same man on the roof as yesterday. He handed it to Reedy, who peered through it.

"Same man as yesterday, long black hair and a gun on his left hip," Jess told him.

"Agreed," said Reedy.

"I'll give you a good half hour to get into position over by the livery. You still got extra cartridges for the Winchester?"

"Both front pockets are full and the bullet loops are full on my holster."

"All right, but when you get into position, don't move to the back of that building until you hear me shoot."

Reedy took the Winchester and slowly made his way through the trees to the end of town. Once he reached it, he calculated it would take him a minute or so to reach the back of the building that was directly across from the livery. He leaned against a tree to keep himself out of sight.

Jess had already chambered a round into the heavy-caliber buffalo rifle. He looked at his pocket watch and saw that a half hour had passed since Reedy left.

He propped the stock of the rifle on a sturdy branch, lifted the ladder sights and rested his cheek on the buttstock. He saw a piece of dried sagebrush rolling along the ground behind the buildings. It rolled past the back of the saloon, giving him a good idea of the wind speed.

He took aim at the man, aiming slightly to one side to counter the wind. As he started putting pressure on the trigger, the back door of the saloon opened. Malone walked out and up the steps to the roof.

He removed his cheek and relaxed as he watched him reach the roof and talk to the man with the long black hair. Malone was standing with his back to Jess as he talked.

"Too bad I can't kill Malone," he said to himself. "The way they're lined up, I could kill 'em both with one shot."

Reedy

Malone stood on the roof with Frenchy for a while. Reedy, standing in his position, kept wondering why Jess hadn't taken the shot yet.

"What the hell is the holdup?" he said, as he peered around the tree at the building he needed to get to.

Jess stood there, the rifle still propped on the branch, waiting for Malone to go back into the saloon. He finally turned and went down the steps to the bottom and went into the saloon. The door shut.

Jess put his cheek on the buttstock again and watched the leaves on the trees at the outer edge to check for wind speed again. The wind seemed to be picking up more.

He adjusted his aim slightly more and slowly squeezed back on the trigger until the rifle bucked and boomed against his shoulder.

The three-hundred-seventy-five-grain slug cut through two leaves before crossing the distance to where Frenchy stood, his back now turned toward Jess.

The slug ripped through Frenchy's body, went through the front wooden façade and hit the wall of the building across the street. Frenchy dropped to the roof like a sack of potatoes.

CHAPTER THIRTY-TWO

As soon as Reedy heard the loud shot, he bolted out of the trees and ran as fast as he could to the back of the building across from the livery.

Walker heard the shot and ran to the front window of the livery, looking nervously toward the saloon. He couldn't see Frenchy on the roof of the saloon anymore. The wind picked up some more, causing dust to be carried a few feet above the street.

He didn't see when Reedy ducked between the buildings across from him. Reedy kept his back to the wall as he moved toward the front. He removed his hat, dropped it on the ground behind him and edged a look around the corner of the building.

When he did, Walker noticed the movement and fired at Reedy at the same instant that Reedy fired at him.

The slug from Walker's rifle grazed Reedy's left arm above his elbow. Reedy's slug hit Walker in his ribs, burning flesh from them and nicking one of the ribs. Reedy didn't even bother to check his arm.

Instead, he fired two more shots through the wall on either side of the open window, hoping to get lucky, but Walker turned, dove backward, and hit the floor on his stomach. He quickly crawled to the other side of the hayloft, dragging his rifle by the barrel.

The wooden shutters on the window started moving with the wind, banging against the wall and the window frame. It almost sounded like gunshots.

Inside the saloon, Malone heard the loud thud Frenchy's body made on the roof a second after he heard the loud gunshot. He ran to the back kitchen and peeked out the window. He didn't see anyone, but he was certain the shot had come from the woods.

He began firing his rifle wildly toward the trees, shooting high and emptying his rifle, hoping for a lucky hit. Jess simply kept his back to the trunk of a large tree. He heard the aimless slugs cutting through branches and leaves, but he knew he was safe.

Jess had heard the gunfire exchange over at the livery. He knew he couldn't kill Malone, but at least he could keep him busy.

Chambering another round into his buffalo rifle, he fired at one of the windows on the second floor of the saloon. Malone heard the window shatter upstairs and grunted.

"Whoever it is, he must think someone is upstairs," he said as he shoved fresh rounds into his rifle.

Malone ran to the front of the saloon and looked down at the livery. He didn't see anyone, but he had heard the gunfire.

He wondered if Walker had been hit and how many men were attacking them.

Jess continued a steady rate of fire with his buffalo rifle, pounding the second floor of the saloon. Then, he loaded his buffalo rifle again, leaned it against the tree and picked up the Winchester.

He fired every round in the rifle, moving back and forth along the upper floor of the saloon, aiming high, praying Malone would stay on the first floor.

Reedy waited and shoved fresh rounds into his rifle and kept peeking around the corner of the building. Frustrated, he decided to risk a run across to the livery.

He fired off three shots and then dashed across the street to the side of the livery, having to dodge a rolling sagebrush as it bounced along the street.

Walker was knelt behind bales of hay, checking his ribs where he had been shot. Reedy, wanting to throw off whoever was in the hayloft, put his back against the wall of the other building next to the livery and fired off three rounds.

Then, he ran to the back of the livery, twenty feet from the back wall. He fired four rounds into the back wall, aiming at nothing in particular.

He ran to the other side of the livery and again, fired off four shots at the building. Walker figured he was surrounded by as many as four men, which is what Reedy wanted him to think.

Walker panicked and threw his rifle off the hayloft. He climbed down the ladder, grabbed his rifle and ran to his

Reedy

horse. He climbed up in the saddle and grabbed the reins to the other two horses.

Heeling his horse, he rode out of the livery and headed to the saloon. He dropped the reins to the two horses on the ground and looked at Malone, who was staring out the front window.

"There's too many of 'em," he shouted. "Git on your horse and get out of here."

"I must have three or four behind the saloon and one of 'em has a heavy-caliber rifle," yelled Malone.

Walker gigged his horse into a dead run toward the other end of the street. Jess heard the horse running and snatched his buffalo rifle. He aimed toward the end of town and waited.

As soon as Walker came into view, Jess took aim ahead of him and fired. Walker's arms flew up in the air as the slug punched into his side. He slid off the side of his horse and rolled a few times on the ground. When he stopped, he wasn't moving.

Reedy ran around to the front of the livery just as Walker fell off his horse at the end of the street and Malone came running out through the batwings. He headed for his horse.

Reedy aimed his rifle at Malone and yelled.

"You're not going anywhere, Malone," he yelled.

Another rush of wind picked up dust that got into Malone's eyes, causing him to blink to try to get the sand out.

Malone, taken by surprise upon hearing the familiar voice, froze in his tracks. He slowly turned to see Reedy holding the rifle high and walking toward him.

"Frank Reedy? This can't be. I done killed you already."

"You came real close, but not close enough."

"I saw the hole in your badge and the blood on your shirt. I took your boots off you and you never moved."

"I was out cold. Didn't come to for quite a while."

"It was you chasing us all along?"

"That's right, me and Jess Williams."

"The bounty hunter?"

"Yep."

Malone still had his rifle in his hands, but hadn't levered a round into it yet. He glared at Reedy and levered a round into the rifle.

"You'll never make it, Malone," Reedy warned him.

"You go to hell, you sonofabitch," he yelled as he raised the rifle up to fire.

Reedy fired first, aiming low on his legs on purpose. The slug slammed into Malone's shin. Malone fired and the slug grazed Reedy's right arm, a few inches below the top of his shoulder.

Malone fell to the ground on his rear and tried to lever another round into his rifle, but Jess suddenly appeared at the corner of the saloon. He fired his Winchester and the slug slammed into the side of Malone's left arm, causing him to drop the rifle.

Reedy and Jess both approached Malone, still sitting in the street, moaning and groaning in pain.

Reedy

"Just kill me and get it over with," he wailed.

"Not a chance of that," said Reedy as he reached him. "I've been shot three times so far trying to get your sorry ass to Calico for your hanging, and I ain't about to end it here."

"Where are the rest of your posse?" Malone asked.

"You're lookin' at 'em," said Jess.

"It was just you two?"

"Yep, just the two of us," said Reedy as he put his left foot out and kicked Malone in the chest, knocking him backward into the dirt.

"Jess, take his pistol," ordered Reedy.

Jess walked over to Malone, reached down and jerked the pistol out of his holster. He pitched it out into the street.

"Roll over on your stomach and put your hands behind your back," Reedy ordered.

Malone rolled over onto his stomach. Jess kept his rifle aimed at the back of Malone's calf, ready to shoot him again.

Reedy reached down, put the manacles on his wrists and stood back up.

"You are officially back in my custody, Ned Malone. Judge Hood is waiting to hang you and we're gonna deliver you alive to him. He just said you had to be alive. He didn't say how many holes we can put in ya, so don't test my patience."

Reedy reached down and jerked Malone to his feet. He shoved him toward the saloon and pushed him through the batwings. Malone limped badly all the way.

Once inside, Reedy pushed him down on his behind at one of the posts holding up the second floor and used a piece of rope to tie around Malone's neck. He tied it tightly to the post.

"That should give you a taste of what's waitin' for you when you get to Calico," Reedy told him.

Jess walked in and glared at Malone. Then, he looked at Reedy.

"I'm going to round up the horses and take 'em to the livery," said Jess. "We can leave for Calico in the morning."

Malone hung his head and moaned in agony, both physical and mental, knowing he was doomed to hang now. He looked at Reedy hatefully.

"Damn you to hell, Frank Reedy," he spat.

"Maybe, but you're going first," he said.

Jess put his bandanna up to block the wind and sand from his mouth. He tilted his head down slightly, trying to keep sand from getting in his eyes.

He gathered all the horses, including his own, and put them in the livery. He went back to the saloon with one set of saddlebags with some food supplies to cook a meal. He lowered his bandanna.

"That wind is gettin' stronger out there," said Jess as he got his medical bag out from the saddlebags.

He bandaged Reedy's two new minor wounds and then wrapped the ones on Malone's shin and arm. After they ate, they took turns at watch, always keeping an eye on Malone.

There would be no more escapes.

CHAPTER THIRTY-THREE

The next morning, after Jess and Reedy ate, Reedy took his boots off Malone and put them back on his own feet, after removing the ones he had taken off Shuster. He left them on the floor and Malone eyeballed them.

"I don't suppose you're gonna let me wear those?" he asked.

Reedy scowled at him.

"Nope, not a chance," he said.

Jess took time to clean and wrap Reedy's two new minor wounds again. Jess had the three horses outside at the hitching post in front of the saloon. He had released Walker's and Frenchy's horses out to roam free.

The wind had died down during the night. The sun was out and it was a crisp, cool, sunny day outside.

He took time to cut some leather straps from a long rolled-up piece he kept in his saddlebags for the purpose of securing bodies to saddles.

Reedy looked over at him.

"We ready?" Reedy asked.

"Yep."

Reedy walked to Malone and untied him from the post. He pulled off one of Malone's socks, the one with dried blood on it from the bullet he had taken to the shinbone. He left the other sock on and Malone frowned.

"Why'd you take one sock?"

Reedy held it up to him.

"This one has your blood on it," he explained. "If I have to tell you to shut up more than once before we get to Calico, I'm gonna shove this in your mouth and gag you for the rest of the trip."

"You are one mean sumbitch, Reedy," he spat.

"Yeah, and I got that way from dealing with killers like you for so many years."

Reedy unlocked the manacles from the post and hauled Malone to his feet. He nodded at Jess, who pulled his Colt out from the front of his holster. He cocked it and aimed it at one of Malone's feet.

"He tries anything funny, shoot him in the foot," said Reedy as he locked the manacles again, this time in the front.

It took them a while, but they got Malone in the saddle. Jess put his pistol away and proceeded to tie Malone's manacled hands to the horn of his saddle.

He tied both of his ankles to the stirrups and ran a rope underneath the belly of the horse, securing the two stirrups together. Reedy looked up at Malone and grinned.

Reedy

"It's gonna be a real uncomfortable ride to Calico for you, so don't do anything that'll make it any more uncomfortable."

"Kiss my ass, you badge-totin' sonofabitch," spat Malone, a hateful expression washing across his face.

Reedy put his finger in the hole of his badge.

"Yeah, well, this badge and the others I had in my pocket saved my life."

"I should have put another slug in your sorry ass."

"Yeah, you should have, but you didn't."

Reedy tied Malone's horse to the back of the saddle on Sharps. He and Jess climbed up in the saddle. Jess looked over at Reedy.

Well, you got shot three times and left for dead once," said Jess. "Was it all worth it?"

Reedy smiled.

"It will be when I watch Judge Hood pull that lever on those gallows after they put that special noose around his neck."

"What do you mean, special noose?" asked Malone.

Reedy turned in the saddle and smiled at him.

"I'm sure the judge will explain it to you before he pulls the lever, but at least it'll give you something to think about on the way to Calico."

Jess started the horses. Malone hung his head, wondering what the special noose was.

***

The ride to Calico was a quiet one. Malone hardly said a word. Reedy only fed him leftover pan bread and water. He had soiled himself and smelled awful, but Reedy wasn't going to take any chance of him attempting to escape again.

Judge John Hood sat in the café by the window, looking over at the crimson red painted gallows. Someone had erected a sign over the stairs going up to the gallows that read, "Welcome to hell, Ned Malone."

When they rode into the town, all the townsfolk who were out pointed and stared at Malone. One man threw a half-eaten apple at him, narrowly missing his head.

Hood heard the commotion. He stood up and walked to the door. He saw Frank Reedy and Jess riding side by side and then he saw Ned Malone on the horse behind Reedy. Malone didn't look up; he kept his head hung low.

Hood stepped out onto the front porch of the café. Reedy pointed to the judge and Jess turned the horses toward him. They rode to him and stopped.

Hood looked at Reedy's arms and the hole in his badge.

"Jeez, Frank, how many times did you get shot?"

"Three, although the last two weren't bad," explained Reedy.

"Looks like you're gonna need a new badge, along with a new shirt."

"I got a dozen new badges back at my office in Stratton."

Hood looked at Jess.

"Thank you for your help, Mr. Williams. I won't forget it either."

"That's good to know, Judge," said Jess.

The town marshal, Randy Clinton, walked over to them.

Reedy

"We can put him in my jail until the hanging," said Clinton.

Hood shook his head.

"No, I'm going to sentence him now and then hang him right after."

Malone finally lifted his head.

"What about my trial?" Malone demanded.

"You're not only guilty of the rape and killing of my wife, Cassie, but also the murder of two Deputy United States Marshals and the attempted murder of U.S. Marshal Frank Reedy, so your trial will be in the saddle you sit in and right now."

"This ain't right," bellowed Malone as the townsfolk gathered around.

Hood looked up at Malone.

"Ned Malone, I find you guilty of multiple murders and heinous crimes," he said in his official tone of voice. "I sentence you to hang by the neck until dead, which should take a little longer than usual."

Hood rapped his knuckles on the wall of the café, signifying the gavel hitting the wooden sound block on his bench. He nodded to two of the men in town, the biggest, strongest men he could find.

"Get his sorry ass off that horse and bring him to me on top of the gallows."

Hood walked to the steps. He smiled inwardly as he read the sign written in the blood red paint over the stairs as he took them one at a time.

The two burly men cut the leather straps and one of them pulled him off the horse. Malone could hardly walk, so the two men literally carried him across the street to the gallows.

Malone groaned when he saw the sign over the steps of the gallows, welcoming him to hell. His feet bounced off the edge of each step as they carried him up.

They reached the top of the gallows and the two men carried Malone to the trap door. They held onto him while the hangman put the rope around his neck and snugged it a little. Malone swallowed the lump of fear in his throat.

The hangman stepped away and the judge stood directly behind Malone. The circuit court judge was on the gallows too. He had already signed the proper and official paperwork for Malone's hanging.

Hood leaned forward and whispered into Malone's ear.

"I have nightmares every night about seeing my poor dead wife's body lying in the undertaker's parlor before we buried her. You took the most important thing in my life away from me and for no real reason. It left a hole in my heart. Pulling the lever on the trap door and watching the life slowly drain from your eyes won't fill that hole, but it might make it a little less painful.

"Now, I want you to know that the noose around your neck was made special just for you. It won't strangle you like a regular noose, but rather, it will tighten slowly. Every time you struggle, it'll tighten a little more, like what a boa constrictor does to its prey.

Reedy

"Also, the trap door is specially designed for you. See, when I pull that lever, you won't fall eight or ten feet so your neck snaps, killing you quickly. It will only drop eight inches, so the noose tightens around your neck more slowly. That way, I can stand in front of you and watch you die."

"Don't I get a black face covering?" Malone asked.

Hood shook his head back and forth slowly.

"No, not you. I want you to see me watching you. If you try to close your eyes, I'll lift them up myself. Are you ready to see what hell really looks like?"

"No, I'm not," said Malone.

"Good," said Hood.

Jess and Reedy sat in the saddle and watched the crowd gather around the gallows.

Jess leaned over toward Reedy.

"Malone looks scared to death," he said.

"Hanging is a hard way to go," said Reedy.

"What is the special noose you mentioned?"

Reedy leaned over and explained about the noose and the short rope that would only drop Malone eight inches.

Jess pressed his lips tightly together and grunted. He looked at Malone's terrified face as the judge put his hand on the lever.

"Well, I can't say he doesn't deserve it," said Jess.

Hood stood there, his hand on the lever for a total of thirty seconds, which seemed like an eternity for Malone, whose eyes were darting around in total fear. Hood moved his hand and Malone's eyes darted down to it.

Then, his eyes slowly lifted to see the judge smiling what could only be described as an evil smile as he jerked the lever.

The floor under Malone's feet flew open. His body dropped a mere eight inches. The noose began tightening more as Malone's legs struggled to find a grip on the edge of the floor.

Hood stood there, gazing into his eyes as the noose got tighter and tighter. The life in Malone's eyes began to drain out, little by little as his feet and legs slowed down their struggling. His body became limp and his eyes became vacant, probably staring at the depths of hell now.

"No one will miss you, Ned Malone, except me, and only because I'd like to hang you a hundred times over," Hood whispered to the dead murderer, hoping he could hear him from the other side of life.

The crowd cheered and clapped and then began dispersing. Jess looked over at the hotel down the street and then at Reedy.

"I'll get us the two best rooms at the hotel and then you can see the doctor in town," suggested Jess.

"That sounds mighty good," said Reedy.

They headed for the livery first and then walked to the hotel. Jess rented the two biggest rooms in the place and then Reedy went to the doctor to have his wounds tended to.

CHAPTER THIRTY-FOUR

Jess and Reedy stayed in Calico for an extra day. They watched as the gallows were dismantled, piece by piece and burned at the end of town. Malone's body was buried at the end of town where a trash hole had been almost filled with rubbish from the townsfolk.

No grave marker was installed. The trash along with his body was covered with five feet of dirt. Judge Hood had thanked both Reedy and Jess numerous times. He went back to work, traveling to his office in Fort Worth, Texas, to commence holding hearings with the court.

Jess agreed to ride back to Stratton with Reedy.

When they arrived, Bodine ran out of his office to greet them.

"I'll be danged Jess," he blurted. "About time you visited. Are you staying for a few days?"

"Yeah, and you and Reedy are gonna stay at my house," said Jess. "We'll go fishing on the lake and relax by the fire in the evening."

"By golly, I'm gonna stop by the fishing camp and buy a new fishing pole," said Bodine.

"You do that," said Jess. "Me and Reedy will ride to the house. I assume there's someone there to take care of the horses?"

"The man Henry has working there now is Buster. You have a barn behind the house that'll hold six horses at a time. Two house workers are staying there all the time. I'll bring some steaks with me when I go there."

"All right then, I'm gonna go talk to Henry at the hotel," said Jess.

Reedy and Jess dismounted and walked to the hotel. When they walked into the beautiful mahogany bar off to one side of the lobby, Henry already had a table set up with glasses and a bottle of fine Tennessee whiskey.

Henry walked to Jess and shook his hand.

"It's really good to see my investment partner," he said. "Come and sit with me for a while."

"My banker in Black Creek tells me you've made us quite a bunch of money," Jess told him as the three sat down.

A waiter came over and poured some of the fine whiskey into their glasses.

"With all the money you gave me to invest, we've continued the construction of homes on the lake. We have judges, congressmen and all sorts of rich and powerful people living around it now. Most only stay a week or two at a time. We've now begun building smaller homes around the lake behind the bigger homes. We're situating them between the other houses so they all have a good view of the water. The hotel on the lake and the fishing camp are both doing great business."

"Sorry you have to do all the work while I run around killing bad men," Jess told him.

"Not to worry," said Henry. "I take a larger percent of profit for myself, which makes up for your absence."

"That seems fair," said Jess.

Henry leaned forward on the table.

"I'm so glad you're here," he said, sounding serious now. "With all the people moving here, we're also getting a lot of poor families, seeking out a better life. But some of them are camped outside of town in tents and some even under lean-tos. We find them work as soon as the jobs come open, but there are just too many people."

"What are you thinking about?" Jess asked.

"I'd like to build a small one-story hotel with a few dozen rooms that can house up to four people at a time. We could let them stay free of charge for one month. It will be a temporary fix and it will keep some people from putting up tents and lean-tos. It doesn't look good for the town."

Jess looked at Frank, and he nodded his head that he agreed.

Jess turned back to Henry.

"How much do you need from me?" he asked.

"If we each toss in a thousand, I can build it. The men in the tents and lean-tos will help with the construction and it will be built behind the hotel on the lake."

"Wire my banker in Black Creek tomorrow and tell him I said it was okay to transfer the money."

"Thanks," said Henry.

They sat there, discussing their business venture and the possibility of expanding to a town nearby. After that, Jess and Reedy left and rode to his house on the lake.

The man working there, Buster, was sitting on the front porch. He stood up.

"Mr. Williams, welcome back to your house," he said as he walked down the steps and took hold of the horses.

"I'll take 'em to the barn," said Jess. "Being a stranger, they won't move for you."

Jess and Reedy dismounted.

Buster followed Jess into the barn and once in their stalls, Buster took care of unsaddling them. He turned to Jess.

"Marshal Bodine is already in the house and he brought a half dozen huge steaks with him," said Buster.

"Good, then we can all eat steak," Jess told him.

"I'm getting a steak?" Buster asked.

"Yep, plus the two house workers," said Jess.

"Everyone's gonna love workin' for you," said Buster.

Jess walked back to the house and found Reedy and Bodine sitting on the porch, sipping whiskey. They had a glass already poured for him. He sat down and sighed as he looked out over the lake. Several boats were out with people fishing.

"This is so peaceful here," said Jess.

Reedy

"You need to come use it more often," said Bodine. "Staying out on the trail for months at a time, hunting killers and the like has got to put a strain on a man."

"I know, but it's hard to stop when I still have a wanted poster in my pocket, wondering who he'll kill next if I don't get to him first."

"Well, ya can't get 'em all, Jess," said Bodine.

"I try. Maybe in the future, it'll be different and killers will be caught before they commit their crimes."

Reedy shook his head.

"Nah, even a hundred years from now, people will kill other people," professed Reedy. "It's just the nature of some men to be evil. They're either born that way or they become evil through some event or events that will happen in their lives. I don't see that changing. Maybe the law will get better at catching them and locking them up, but there will always be bad men."

"I think you're right, Frank," said Jess.

One of the women walked out from the house.

"Mr. Williams, how many steaks should we prepare?"

"All six," he said.

"All six?"

"You two are joining us for supper, along with Buster."

"That's very generous of you, Mr. Williams," she said.

Buster came around the corner of the house just as Melvin the delivery boy came around the other corner.

"I'll have those boats ready for you men to go fishing in the morning," announced Buster.

"No, you won't," challenged Melvin. "That's my job."

Buster shrugged his shoulders.

"Fine with me, Melvin," he said.

Melvin walked up the steps and shook hands with Jess.

"Nice to see you again, Mr. Williams," said Melvin.

Jess shook his hand and smiled at him.

"I heard you've become quite the businessman in town," said Jess.

"Yes, I have, and that brings me to part of my business," said Melvin.

"And, what might that be?" Jess asked him.

Reedy chuckled knowingly.

"Well, I have to inform you and Mr. Stratton that the cost of supplying firewood goes up five percent next month," Melvin explained with a serious look on his face.

Jess smiled at him.

"Isn't that a little steep for one raise?"

"I need new gloves once in a while and a new file to sharpen my axe and those things cost money, you know," debated Melvin.

Jess looked over at Reedy, who was still chuckling.

"I thought you said he was becoming a good businessman?"

"He is," said Reedy. "He just raised your prices for firewood and you haven't been at your house for a half hour yet."

Jess looked at Melvin with one eye half closed.

Reedy

"You gonna bring me good firewood, like red and white oak?" Jess asked him.

"Of course," said Melvin.

"Cut to the right length?"

"Longer for the outdoor fire in the yard and slightly shorter for the hearths inside and even shorter for the cookstoves in the kitchen," Melvin stated bluntly.

Jess leaned back in his chair.

"Then, five percent it is," agreed Jess.

Melvin nodded and took off running. Reedy looked over at Jess, grinning widely.

"What?" Jess asked.

"Henry gives him new gloves when he needs them and he has Melvin's axe sharpened every day for free."

"Really?" asked Jess. "But he said those things cost money."

"Yeah, but he never said who was payin' for 'em."

Jess looked over at the corner where Melvin had disappeared.

"Why that little conniving shit," said Jess.

"That's what I call him," chuckled Reedy.

"Enough of that," said Bodine. "I'm bettin' five bucks that I'll catch the biggest fish tomorrow."

Jess turned to him with his open hand out.

"You want to pay me now and get it over with?" Jess asked him.

"Heck, no," said Bodine. "See, while you've been out chasing bad men around, I've been out there finding all the sweet spots on the lake. And I've got me a new fishin' pole too."

"We'll see about that tomorrow morning," said Jess. "Now, let's go inside and eat those steaks."

"Oh, about that," said Bodine. "I was thinkin' you might want to reimburse me for the steaks?"

Jess turned to him and grinned.

"I will, with the five bucks I'm gonna win from you tomorrow," Jess told him.

They all went inside. The women had the table all set and ready. They ate supper and laughed and joked for hours. During a few seconds of silence between laughs, Jess glanced down at his front pocket where he had two folded wanted posters.

He knew that in a few days, he'd be back on the trail, hunting the men down, but for now, he would enjoy his friends and his huge house on the lake. He looked up from his pocket when they all started laughing again. He smiled as he looked around the table.

There would be time to continue the hunt…later.

The End

*Please visit **www.jesswilliamswesterns.com** the official Jess Williams website where you can sign up to be notified of the next book coming out and join the discussion group.*

Read the Entire Series of Jess Williams Westerns (Listed in Order)…

1. *The Reckoning*
2. *Brother's Keeper*
3. *Sins of The Father*
4. *The Burning*
5. *The Dodge City Massacre*
6. *Hell Hath No Fury*
7. *The River Runs Red*
8. *Death Dance*
9. *Blood Trail*
10. *Badge of Honor*
11. *Long Guns*
12. *Wanted*
13. *Tin Man*
14. *Retribution*
15. *Hired Gun*
16. *Hunted*
17. *Resurrection*
18. *In Cold Blood*
19. *Reagan's Riders*
20. *The Bounty*
21. *Wagon Train*
22. *The Killing*
23. *Hombre*
24. *Body Count*
25. *Hunt Down*
26. *From the Grave*
27. *Black Raven*
28. *The Bounty Hunters*
29. *To Hell and Back*
30. *Machete*
31. *Streets of Laredo*
32. *Ride of Revenge*
33. *Cold Justice*
34. *God's Gun*

35. *Dark Cloud*
36. *Redemption*
37. *Trouble In Navarro*
38. *Black Heart*
39. *The Journey*
40. *The Transport*
41. *Painted Ladies*
42. *Range War*
43. *Crossroads*
44. *Death By Lead*
45. *Dundee*
46. *A Christmas Miracle*
47. *Old Guns*
48. *Wildcat*
49. *Hades*
50. *Fool's Gold*
51. *Devil's Due*
52. *The Kid*
53. *Gold Fever*
54. *Lone Wolf*
55. *Sister's Keeper*
56. *Medicine Man*
57. *Shane*
58. *Chasing Evil*
59. *Stratton*
60. *Good Deeds and Bad Seeds*
61. *Deadly Matters*
62. *Return of Wildcat*
63. *Outlaw Havens*
64. *The Chase*
65. *Gunslinger's Dream*
66. *Greed*
67. *Ambushed*
68. *Double Revenge*
69. *Black Creek*
70. *Mysterious Ways*
71. *Hell Town*
72. *Deadly Pursuit*
73. *Close Calls*
74. *Triple Trouble*
75. *Lead Jury*
76. *The Apprentice*
77. *The Guardian*
78. *Schoolmarm*
79. *Berkshire*
80. *Wounded*
81. *Justice Reigns*
82. *Red*
83. *The Ranch Hand*
84. *The Boone Gang*
85. *Against All Odds*
86. *Nellie's Revenge*
87. *The Gauntlet*
88. *Oklahoma Outlaws*

89. *Payback*
90. *The Plot*
91. *Taking Sides*
92. *Devil or Angel*
93. *The Rundown*
94. *Martha Heller*
95. *Bad Men*
96. *Oden's End*
97. *The Notorious Four*
98. *Stealing Apples*
99. *John Smith*
100. *Calcutta*
101. *A Sister's Burden*
102. *Rescued*
103. *The Border*
104. *The Promise*
105. *Left For Dead*
106. *Chakits*
107. *Cheyenne*
108. *Three Good Men*
109. *Salvation*
110. *The Long Ride to Justice*
111. *The Mission*
112. *Martha*
113. *Sam Smith*
114. *Noah Brown*
115. *Second Chances*
116. *Fresh Graves*

Coming soon…the next book in the Jess Williams Western series.

The first three books in the series are available as a set. Visit Amazon for ***"The Trilogy"*** *and other box sets of Jess Williams Westerns.*

Also look for ***"Wanted & Wanted II, A Western Story Collection"*** *by Robert J. Thomas and other western authors.* ***"The Shepherd"*** *and* ***"Damsel In Distress"*** *are short stories in the collection, written by Robert J. Thomas and featuring Jess Williams.*

Other books available by Robert J. Thomas…

Neversafe

Made in the USA
Monee, IL
07 February 2023

27088956R00156